Etgar Keret was bor[n] ... fifteen stories in *Gaz[a]* ... best of his short fict[ion] ... *Missing Kissinger, Kn[...]* ... *Anihu*. All his works have been bestsellers ... and his work has been translated into fourteen languages to date. He has also written comic books and screenplays. His movies *Red Heart* and *Skin Deep* have won Israeli Oscars. He lectures at Tel Aviv University's School of Film.

Samir El-youssef was born in 1965 in Lebanon. He was brought up in Rashidia refugee camp in southern Lebanon. His first collection of short stories *Domestic Affairs* was published in Beirut in 1994 in Arabic by AISP. A new collection of stories *Afternoon of Silence* was published in 2003 in Arabic by Merit, in Cairo. His literary study of the Palestinian writer Ghassan Kanafani is forthcoming from Biann Press in Beirut. He writes regularly for *Al Hayat* and other Arab newspapers and literary journals worldwide. He holds a master's degree in philosophy from Birkbeck College, University of London. He lives in London.

GAZA BLUES

DIFFERENT STORIES

GAZA BLUES
DIFFERENT STORIES

Etgar Keret and Samir El-youssef

DAVID
PAUL

First published in Great Britain 2004

By David Paul
29 Redston Road, London N8 7HL
www.davidpaulbooks.com

Worldwide distribution (except North America) by Central Books,
99 Wallis Road, London, E9 5LN

A CIP catalogue of this book is available from the British Library

The Day the Beast Got Thirsty © Samir El-youssef

Copyright credits for Etgar Keret are on acknowledgements page

ISBN 0-9540542-4-5

Cover design: Raanan Elizov

Printed and bound in Great Britain by
Biddles Ltd, King's Lynn, Norfolk

Contents

Etgar Keret

CRAMPS

That night I dreamt that I was a forty-year-old woman, and my husband was a retired colonel. He was running a community centre in a poor neighbourhood, and his social skills were shit. His workers hated him, because he kept yelling at them. They complained that he treated them like they were in basic training. Every morning I'd make him an omelette, and for supper a veal cutlet with mashed potatoes. When he was in a decent mood, he'd say the food tasted good. He'd never clear the table. Once a month or so, he'd bring home a bouquet of dead flowers that immigrant kids used to sell at an intersection where the lights were really slow.

That night I dreamt that I was a forty-year-old woman, and that I was having cramps, and it's night-time, and suddenly I realise I'm all out of tampons, and I try to wake my husband, who's a retired colonel, and ask him to go to the all-night pharmacy or to drive me there at least, because I don't have a driving licence, and even if I did, we still have an army car, and I'm not allowed to drive it. I told him it was an emergency, but he wouldn't go, just kept mumbling in his sleep, saying the meal was lousy, and that the cooks could forget about leave; because this was the army and not some fucking summer camp. I covered myself with a folded tissue, and tried to lie on my back without breathing, so I wouldn't drip. But my whole body hurt, and the blood was gushing out of me, sounding like a broken sewage pipe. It leaked over my hips, and my legs, and splashed over my stomach. And the tissue turned into a wad that stuck to my hair and my skin.

That night I dreamt that I was a forty-year-old woman and that I was disgusted with myself, with my life. With not having a driving licence, with not knowing English, with never being abroad. The blood that had dripped all over me was beginning to harden, and I felt like it was a kind of a curse. Like my period would never end.

That night I dreamt that I was a forty-year-old woman, and that I fell asleep, and dreamt I was a twenty-seven-year-old man who gets his wife pregnant again, and then finishes medical school and forces her and the baby to join him when he goes to do his residency abroad. They suffer terribly. They don't know a word of English. They don't have any friends, and it's cold outside, and snowing. And then, one Sunday, I take them on a picnic and spread out the blanket on the lawn, and they take the food from their picnic baskets and put out the food they've brought. And after we finish eating, I take out a shotgun and shoot them like dogs. The policemen come to my house. The finest detectives in the police force try to get me for murder. They put me in this room, they yell at me, they won't let me smoke, they won't let me go to the toilet, but I don't break. And my husband in bed beside me keeps yelling, "I don't give a damn how you did it before. I'm the commander around here now."

CRAZY GLUE

She said, "Don't touch that."

"What is it?" I asked.

"It's glue," she said. "Special glue. The best kind."

"What did you buy it for?"

"Because I need it," she said. "A lot of things around here need gluing."

"Nothing around here needs gluing," I said. "I wish I understood why you buy all this stuff."

"For the same reason I married you," she murmured. "To help pass the time."

I didn't want to fight, so I kept quiet, and so did she.

"Is it any good, this glue?" I asked. She showed me the picture on the box, with this guy hanging upside-down from the ceiling.

"No glue can really make a person stick like that," I said. "They just took the picture upside-down. They must have put a lamp on the floor." I took the box from her and peered at it. "And there, look at the window. They didn't even bother to hang the blinds the other way. They're upside-down, if he's really standing on the ceiling. Look," I said again, pointing to the window. She didn't look.

"It's eight already," I said. "I've got to run." I picked up my briefcase and kissed her on the cheek. "I'll be back pretty late. I'm working —"

"Overtime," she said. "Yes, I know."

I called Abby from the office.

"I can't make it today," I said. "I've got to get home early."

"Why?" Abby asked. "Something happen?"

"No ... I mean, maybe. I think she suspects something."

There was a long silence. I could hear Abby's breathing on the other end.

"I don't see why you stay with her," she whispered. "You never do anything together. You don't even fight. I'll never understand it." There was a pause, and then she repeated, "I wish I understood." She was crying.

"I'm sorry. I'm sorry, Abby. Listen, someone just came in," I lied. "I've got to hang up. I'll come over tomorrow. I promise. We'll talk about everything then."

I got home early. I said "Hi" as I walked in, but

there was no reply. I went through all the rooms in the house. She wasn't in any of them. On the kitchen table I found the tube of glue, completely empty. I tried to move one of the chairs, to sit down. It didn't budge. I tried again. Not an inch. She'd glued it to the floor. The fridge wouldn't open. She'd glued it shut. I didn't understand what was happening, what would make her do such a thing. I didn't know where she was. I went into the living room to call her mother's. I couldn't lift the receiver; she'd glued that too. I kicked the table and almost broke my toe. It didn't even budge.

And then I heard her laughing. It was coming from somewhere above me. I looked up, and there she was, standing barefoot on the living room ceiling.

I stared open-mouthed. When I found my voice I could only ask, "What the hell... are you out of your mind?"

She didn't answer, just smiled. Her smile seemed so natural, with her hanging upside-down like that, as if her lips were just stretching on their own by the sheer force of gravity.

"Don't worry, I'll get you down," I said, hurrying to the shelf and grabbing the largest books. I made a tower of encyclopaedia volumes and clambered on top of the pile.

"This may hurt a little," I said, trying to keep my balance. She went on smiling. I pulled as hard as I could, but nothing happened. Carefully, I climbed down.

"Don't worry," I said. "I'll get the neighbours or something. I'll go next door and call for help."

"Fine," she laughed. "I'm not going anywhere."

I laughed too. She was so pretty, and so incongruous, hanging upside-down from the ceiling that way. With her long hair dangling downwards, and her breasts moulded like two perfect teardrops under her white T-shirt. So pretty. I climbed back up onto the pile of books and kissed her. I felt her tongue on mine. The books tumbled out from under my feet, but I stayed floating in mid-air, hanging just from her lips.

FOR ONLY 9.99
(INCL.TAX AND POSTAGE)

Nachum happened on the ad completely by chance, somewhere between the daily horoscope and the sex toys. "Ever wonder about the meaning of life?" the ad enquired. "Ever ask yourself why we exist in the first place?" And it went on to provide the solution: "The answer to this difficult question is right at your fingertips. You'll find it in a small but incredible booklet. In simple and readable language you will find out why you have been placed on this earth. The booklet, printed on the finest paper, complete with enlightening, breathtaking color photographs, will be mailed to your home, beautifully gift-wrapped, for only 9.99!" There was a photograph of a man with glasses reading a small booklet, and smiling happily to himself. And right over his head, in the spot where his thought-bubble should have been, was the inscription, in thick lettering: "The booklet that will change your life!" Nachum was deeply impressed by the picture in the ad. The man looked very happy, and Nachum was also taken in by his broad shoulders, almost like the smiling strongman in the ad for "The Physique of Hercules in only thirty seconds a day, with our new and improved formula. Only 19.99! (incl. tax and postage)." To think that they were offering him the meaning of life. And at half the price!

Nachum's hands shook as he stuck the stamp on the envelope. He knew that the next few days would be the longest ever. The meaning of life was something that had worried him for as long as he could remember, and even though his life was reasonably pleasant and happy, he'd always felt there was something missing. But now, in just a few days, his world would be complete. When he tried to explain to his father the intense curiosity that was welling up within him, he encountered some difficulties. "You're such a moron. Every time some two-timing swindler decides to cash in, all he needs is to place an ad, and my nincompoop of a son sends him the money."

"But Dad, they're not two-timing swindlers," Nachum tried to explain. "The ad even says that if I'm not completely satisfied, I have fourteen days to send the booklet back, and they'll reimburse me. Minus the postage, of course."

Nachum's dad gave a creepy snigger, and his nervous expression became downright menacing.

Placing his hand on Nachum's shoulder, he whispered in a conspiratorial voice: "Know what? Let's put one over on 'em. Let's read the booklet together, and then, once we've figured out the meaning of life, we'll send it back. That'll screw them good. So whaddya say?"

Nachum didn't say anything, though he couldn't help thinking it was very dishonest. He didn't want to upset his dad. But the clamp on his shoulder was growing tighter and tighter. Apparently, his dad had managed to get upset all on his own.

"You imbecile," he shouted. "I'll show you the meaning of life, you piece of defective goods," he ranted on, struggling to pull off his slipper.

"Leave the boy alone," Nachum's mother rushed to his rescue, trying to separate him from his dad.

"Boy?" Nachum's dad wheezed madly, waving the slipper at them like he was about to use it. "He'll be twenty-eight in August."

"So he's a bit naïve," his mother whimpered. "So what?"

Nachum's friends thought it was a scam too. Even Ronit. So, having nobody to share his impatient wait with, he impatiently waited all by himself. The notice from the post office arrived three days later, and Nachum barely managed to grab it from his dad, who was about to swallow it in one of his fits of rage. As soon as he had the package in his hands, even before he'd left the post office, Nachum tore open the brown-paper wrapping and began reading the booklet on his way home. The secret of the human condition was revealed to him, becoming clearer and clearer with every page he read. The incredible booklet was written in such plain and simple language, that Nachum could understand everything without having to reread it (except one part where he had to refer to the breathtaking colour photographs, which really were enlightening, just like the ad said. And by the time he got back to the building where he lived, he knew, for the first time in his life, why he had been placed in this wonderful world of ours, why all of us are here. And a feeling of sublime joy swept over him, a joy mingled with just a tinge of sorrow, for all those years that he'd been forced to live in ignorance. Determined to ensure that others would not have to suffer those tormenting moments of confusion, Nachum raced upstairs, and the very thought that in just a few short seconds he would share the secret of the human condition with his parents brought tears to his eyes – tears which were soon to turn into tears of frustration. His father screamed that he would have no part of this ridiculous farce. And while his mother did listen to his explanations, and looked at his pictures and nodded, her eyes were glazed over, and her nod was hollow. Clearly, she wasn't thinking about the booklet at all. She just wanted to make Nachum feel better.

The next few hours left Nachum feeling frustrated and sad. A quick glance at the newspaper was enough to remind him just how foreign the essence of the human condition was to most of humanity. All those wars, and murders, and ecological disasters, even the drops in the stock market – all those things grew out of ignorance, mistakes caused by a basic failure to understand what life was really about. Mistakes which could be corrected so easily, if only they would listen. But nobody was prepared to listen. Not his relatives, not his friends, not even Ronit. With every fibre of his being Nachum felt the disillusionment. But suddenly, just above the array of easy-loan ads, he caught sight of a familiar face – the man with the broad shoulders and the glasses. Except that in this ad he was talking with a stern-looking man who seemed to be listening very closely. "People don't listen to you?" the ad asked. "Family and close friends pay no attention? We have the solution. For 9.99 we will send you a remarkable booklet, which will teach you how to win over even the most indifferent listener." Nachum could hardly contain his joy. Just as he had reached the verge of despair, everything was about to change. The time spent waiting for the booklet was filled with eager anticipation, and after four interminable days, he held the package in his hands. With bated breath he read the edifying principles, and when he'd finished, he approached his dad, confident that this time he would listen.

Matters progressed at a dizzying pace. Nachum knew the existential truth, and how to cause people to listen to him. The meaning of life was passed on by word of mouth, from one friend to another. It's hard to imagine Nachum's elation as he looked into his mother's glistening eyes, or listened to the delighted laughter of all his friends, especially Ronit. But not everything went smoothly. A couple of orthodox kids, including the grandson of the rabbi of Ludvor, came to visit Nachum at his home, and wanted him to explain the meaning of life to them. Nachum was glad to oblige, and even served them some lemonade. They thanked him politely and left. Nachum didn't give it a second thought. Lots of strangers came to visit him at his home at that point, and those boys were no different.

But the next day hundreds of orthodox people surrounded his home and filled his yard, singing religious hymns like "Son of Lilith, fear our sword – we shall prevail, so quoth the Lord" and "Heathens shall be smitten". Listening to their chants, Nachum knew he was in trouble. He managed to sneak out through the bathroom window and to hide in an abandoned shelter not far from his home. Every morning, Ronit would bring him some sandwiches and a Thermos of coffee. She'd wrap the sandwiches in newsprint, which is how Nachum discovered that the rabbi of Ludvor's grandson had organised a mass departure of students from the yeshivas of Jerusalem, on the grounds that there was no point in seeking the truth in the sacred books, now that it was out in the open. The orthodox community held Nachum personally responsible for the whole thing. And as if things weren't bad enough, his father, whose understanding of the meaning of life did not seem to have changed him much, managed to make things even worse. By finding unconventional uses for cans of baby carrots, he had sent the cantor of the Ludvor congregation into intensive care.

Nachum was keen on making the Chief Rabbi of the Ludvor congregation realise it was just a misunderstanding, and to explain to him that the meaning of life as he had presented it was devoid of any anti-religious implications. Quite the contrary. He himself, after all, made a point of fasting on Yom Kippur and eating matzah every Passover. He'd even received a sports bike for his bar mitzvah like any good Jewish boy. But every time he tried calling the rabbi from the phone booth nearby, the rabbi would just mutter his *Shma Yisrael*, call out for help in Yiddish and hang up before Nachum could say anything. Nachum was growing despondent. He was beginning to feel the effect of the persistent siege on his home and the public denunciation by the rabbis, not to mention the mildew in the shelter and his powerful craving for his mother's cooking. But it was then, just when everything seemed to be going wrong, that it all changed, thanks to Tuesday's tuna fish sandwich. One of the stories in the sandwich wrapping was an interview with the Ludvor cantor, who'd been discharged after making a complete recovery from the canned goods attack, and right above it Nachum spotted an ad. It showed the same broad-shouldered guy, except that this time he was in an awkward position. Right opposite him was a bearded giant, holding a sharp axe, in a menacing pose. The guy with the glasses was giving him a piercing look, reinforced with a dotted line. The ad went like this: "Do you have any enemies? Anyone who wants to harm you? Don't worry! For 9.99 you can own our new booklet, Turn Enemies into 'Friends in Seven Easy Lessons', and learn how to turn negative energies into positive ones with just one look!"

Nachum lost no time sending in his money, and soon the booklet arrived. He read it breath-lessly, and began practising by applying its rules to the misanthropic rats in the shelter. In no time at all, they turned into his friends. Nachum shaved, using the cold water of the shelter, and did his best to iron his clothes. He bought a yarmulke in the nearby used-clothing shop, and set out on his long journey to the residence of the rabbi of Ludvor. Despite his efforts to maintain a low profile, Nachum, for reasons which were not clear to him, drew a great deal of attention. When he reached the rabbi's residence, the crowd was ready for a lynch, but his friends the rats, who'd followed him around by the dozen, protected him. The rabbi came out onto the balcony to find out what was causing the commotion, and sure enough, all it took was one look from Nachum to make him realise there had been a misunderstanding. "Stop," he cried from the balcony high above. "Can't you see that you are facing the Messiah himself, and that he brings us the word of God?" And the crowd looked and could see. That very evening, they held a banquet. Nachum's father and the cantor of Ludvor danced together, arm in arm, as Nachum's rat-friends drank themselves senseless.

From then on, it was not long before the meaning of life could be explained to the rest of humanity. The secret of human existence spread like a virus, and Nachum took the trouble to explain it personally on both of his Nightline appearances. Every country in the world agreed to disarm, some beating their swords into ploughshares, and others finding even better applications. Nachum spent most of his time growing tomatoes in the little garden he cultivated in the backyard of his parents' apartment building, basking in the knowledge that he too had played a role in the happiness of the entire world. There was just one thought that continued to worry him though: the thought of death. It hadn't bothered him in the past, but now that everything was so wonderful, it horrified him. Which is why Nachum was so thrilled when his father drew his attention to an ad in one of the dailies, where the broad-shouldered guy with the glasses, who was looking younger than ever, promised "… a colorful booklet that will show you the way to immortality. All you need is fifteen seconds a day of exercising your sphincter muscles. For only 29.99."

"D'you see that?" Nachum's father grumbled. "One lucky break, and already they go and up the price.

GAZA BLUES

Weisman had a rasping cough, hacking away as if he had tuberculosis, and the whole way there he kept coughing, and spitting into tissues. "It's the cigarettes," he said apologetically. "They're just killing me." When we reached the Erez roadblock, we parked the car at the gas station. There was a taxi waiting for us there, with a local number-plate. "Did you remember to bring the forms?" Weisman asked and spat a yellow gob on the pavement. I nodded. "How about the powers of attorney?" Weisman kept at it. I said yes, those too. We didn't have to tell the driver anything. He knew to take us straight to Fadid's office. It was late May already, but the streets were flooded. Must have been some problem with the sewers.

"Shitty road," the driver complained. "Every three week, tyres finish." I figured he must be setting the stage to hike the price.

We walked into Fadid's office, and he shook our hands. "Let me introduce you," Weisman said, "This is Niv, a junior clerk in our firm. He's here to learn."

"Keep your eyes open, Niv," Fadid said to me in perfect Hebrew. "Keep your eyes open wide and look around you. There's a lot to learn here." Fadid led us into his office. "You sit here," he told Weisman, pointing to the leather chair behind the desk. "And this," he pointed to a small wooden stool in the corner, "this is for the interpreter. I'll be back at two. Make yourselves at home." I sat down on the leather couch in the office and laid out the forms in five separate piles on the low table beside me. Meanwhile, the interpreter arrived too.

"There are five cases," he said. His name was Mas'oud or something. "Two eye, two leg, one ball." From the way Weisman had described it, it wouldn't take more than twenty minutes to get the forms signed for each case plus an interview, which meant that in an hour and a half tops we'd be heading back. Weisman asked them the usual questions through the interpreter, and chain-smoked. I had them sign the medical secrecy waivers and powers of attorney and explained to each of them through the interpreter that if they won our cut was between fifteen and twenty percent. One of them, a half-blind woman, signed with her thumb, like in the movies. The guy who got it in the balls asked in Hebrew, when I'd finished explaining, if the security service guy who kicked his balls in would wind up in jail if we won.

"I know his name and I don't afraid to say it in court," he said. "Steve, *in'al abu*, that was his name." The interpreter told him off in Arabic for talking Hebrew.

"If you want to talk with them yourself," he said, "you don't need me. I can wait outside." I know a little Arabic. Took it in high school.

An hour and ten minutes later we were back in the taxi already, and on our way to the Erez roadblock. Fadid had invited us for lunch, but Weisman explained that we were in a hurry. Weisman didn't stop coughing and spitting into his tissues the whole way back. "Is no good mister," the driver told him. "You should go to doctor. My sister husband he doctor. Live near here."

"No thanks, I'm okay. I'm used to it," Weisman tried to smile at him. "It's all on account of the cigarettes. They're doing me in, like that, slowly."

We hardly spoke the whole way home. I was thinking about my five o'clock basketball practice. "In four of the cases, we stand a chance," Weisman said. "Except the one with the balls. For the whole three years he spent in jail after the interrogation there's no mention of his injury. Go prove that they did it to him three and a half years ago."

"But you're taking him on anyway?" I asked.

"Yeah," Weisman mumbled. "I didn't say I wouldn't take him on. I just said we don't stand a chance." He kept fiddling with the radio dial, trying to pick up something, but all he got was static. After that he tried humming something, but a few seconds later he got bored, lit up and started coughing again. Then he asked me once more if I'd remembered to have them sign everything. I said I had.

"You know what," he turned to me suddenly. "I should have been born black. Every time I come back from this place, I tell myself: 'Weisman, you should have been born black.' Not here, somewhere far away, like New Orleans maybe." He opened the car window and flicked out the cigarette. "Billy, that's what my name should have been. Billy Whiteman, that's a good name for a singer." He cleared his throat as though he were about to start singing, but soon as he inhaled he started coughing and wheezing.

"See this?" he said when he was finished, and showed me the used tissue up close, the one he'd coughed into. "It's something I composed myself. Strong stuff, eh? 'Billy Whiteman and the Dismals', that's what they'd call my band. We'd sing nothing but blues."

Missing Kissinger

She says I don't really love her. I say I do, I think
I do, but I don't. I've heard of people who say they
don't love somebody, but to decide for somebody
else if they love them? That's a new one on me.
True, I had it coming. If you go to bed with a
skunk you shouldn't cry when your kids stink. For
six months already she's been driving me nuts,
sticking her fingers into her cunt after fucking to
see if I really came, and instead of telling her off,
all I say is, "It's okay, darling, we're all a little
insecure." So now she wants to split up, because
she's decided I don't love her. What can I tell her?
If I yell at her not to be so stupid and to stop fucking with my head, she'll only take it as proof.

"Do something to prove to me that you love
me," she says. What does she want me to do?
What? All she has to do is tell me. But she won't.
Because if I really loved her I would know by
myself. What she is prepared to do, is to give me a

clue, or to say what it isn't. Either - or, I can choose. So I told her to say what it isn't, then I'd know something, at least. I wouldn't understand a thing from her clues, that's for sure. "What it's not," she says, "is it's not anything connected to mutilating yourself, like poking out your eye or cutting off your ear, because then you'd be harming someone I love, and indirectly me too. Harming someone close is definitely not a proof of love."

The truth is, I would never touch myself even if she didn't say so. What's poking your eye out got to do with love anyway? And what is that something? That she's not prepared to say, only that doing it to my father or my brothers and sisters is no good either. I give up, and say to myself that it's no use, nothing will help me. Or her either. If you ask stoned blacks riddles you'll wake up with your bones broken. But later on, when we're fucking and she stares deep into my eyes with a concentrated look - she never closes her eyes when we fuck, so I won't push somebody else's tongue into her mouth - I suddenly understand, it comes to me in a flash. "Is it my mother?" I ask, and she refuses to answer me.

"If you really love me then you know for yourself." And after she tastes the fingers she retrieves from her cunt she blurts out: "And don't bring me an ear or a finger or anything like that. It's her heart I want, you hear? Her heart."

I travel all the way to Petah-Tikva with the knife, two buses. A meter and a half long knife, it takes up two seats. I had to buy a ticket for it. What wouldn't I do for her, what wouldn't I do for you, baby? I walked all the way down Stampfer with the knife on my back like some Arab suicide bomber. My mother knew I was coming, so she prepared food for me, with seasoning from hell, like only she knows how to season food. I eat in silence, I haven't got a bad word to say. If you eat sabras with the thorns on, you shouldn't complain when you get piles.

"And how's Miri?" asks my mother. "Is she all right, the darling? Still sticking her chubby fingers into her cunt?"

"She's all right," I say, "she's fine. She asked for your heart. You know, so as to know if I love her."

"Take her Baruch's," my mother laughs, "she'll never notice."

"Oh, mother!" I say, annoyed. "We're not into all those lies. Miri and I are into honesty."

"Good," my mother sighs, "so take her mine. I don't want you to fight on my account, which reminds me, what about your proof to your mother who loves you and who you love back a little bit too?" I slap Miri's heart down on the table in a rage. Why don't they believe me? Why are they always testing me? And now I'll have to take two buses back with this knife, and my mother's heart.

And she probably won't be at home, she'll go back to her ex again. Not that I'm blaming anyone, only myself. There are two kinds of people, the ones that like sleeping next to the wall, and the ones that like sleeping next to the people who push them off the bed.

THE SON OF THE HEAD OF THE MOSSAD

The son of the Head of the Mossad didn't even know he was the son of the Head of the Mossad. He thought his dad had an earth-moving business. And when his dad used to pull the snub-nosed Beretta out of his bottom drawer every morning and check the .38 calibre bullets one by one, he thought it was because he spent so much time working with Arabs from the West Bank. The son of the Head of the Mossad had long skinny legs and a funny name. They called him Oleg, after a friend of his dad's who was killed in the Six-Day War, and in the summertime, whenever you saw him in shorts, staggering on those two skinny white stilts of his, you thought that he was about to topple over any second. And there was that name of his, Oleg. He seemed such an unlikely candidate for son of the Head of the Mossad that sometimes you couldn't help asking yourself whether it wasn't just another stunt that his

father, the Head of the Mossad, had thought up to
disguise his true identity.

There were days when the Head of the Mossad
didn't leave the house. Other days, he'd get home
very late. On those days, when he'd get home, he'd
give a tired smile to the son of the Head of the
Mossad and to his mother, and say: "What a day I
had, don't ask." And they didn't, they just went on
watching TV or doing homework. Even if they
asked him, he wouldn't have answered anyway.

The son of the Head of the Mossad had a girlfriend. Her name was Gabi. They'd talk together
about everything. He and Gabi did most of their
talking lying on the floor in his room. They'd form
a T, with Gabi's head on the stomach of the son of
the Head of the Mossad. Gabi's mother died when
she was a baby, but she told Oleg that she could
actually remember being breast-fed. The son of
the Head of the Mossad said that his earliest
memory was when he was about two and a half.
They were in the car, and someone was honking
like crazy behind them, and his dad was at the
wheel, serene as a Buddha. "They can honk till
hell freezes over, for all I care, Aviva," he said in
his serene voice. "They'll give up in the end," and,
"he can cry till hell freezes over too, for all I care.
He'll give up in the end too." Gabi used to have a
different boyfriend, Simon. Simon had been in
their class in high school, but they threw him out

when he was sixteen, and he went to work for his dad, because he'd thrown a brick at Sylvia, the vice-principal. Simon's father was an earth-mover too, and he couldn't stand the Head of the Mossad. "Everyone's always talking about the contracts his company won," he told Simon once, "but I've never once seen him on a bulldozer, getting a single project off the ground." Simon and his dad thought there was something fishy going on, like the company of the Head of the Mossad was getting paid by the government for work it wasn't really doing. A thought that certainly had a leg to stand on. And if you add the fact that the son of the Head of the Mossad stole Simon's girlfriend from him, it's pretty easy to understand why Simon hated the son of the Head of the Mossad in the worst possible way.

Once, the son of the Head of the Mossad was playing basketball at the sports centre. He went there with his friend Ehud. Ehud was tall and strong, and was always quiet. Lots of people thought Ehud was quiet because he was stupid. That wasn't true. He may not have been the smartest kid around, but he was no moron either. In some ways, Ehud was better suited to be the son of the Head of the Mossad than his real son was. His cool-headedness and his inner calm were just two of the qualities that made him the ideal candidate. And sure enough, the Head of the Mossad liked Ehud a lot. Whenever Ehud came over, the Head of the Mossad would give him a man-to-man slap on the back and say: "What's up, big guy?" And Ehud would smile and keep quiet. It was really out of character. The Head of the Mossad never gave the son of the Head of the Mossad a slap on the back, for example. He never gave a slap on the back to anyone except Ehud and the deputy chief of intelligence, and even then it was only because the two of them had been in officers' training together and had a two-digit list of the times they'd saved each other's lives. When it started getting dark, they stopped playing, and the son of the Head of the Mossad headed home. Ehud stayed behind on the court after everyone had left, so he could practise shooting baskets, as usual.

The son of the Head of the Mossad walked through the playground, and looked at the old swings and ladders. There was nobody there, because it was already getting dark. Nobody except Simon, who was sitting on the edge of the sandpit, looking like he'd had too much to drink. Simon was very down that night, partly because he'd wrecked one of his dad's bulldozers, but mainly because he'd discovered that his sister was fucking one of the Arab workers. He'd had five beers by then and felt like he was going to throw up. The son of the Head of the Mossad walked by, very close to Simon, without even noticing that Simon was Simon, because Simon's face was in the dark, whereas the face of the son of the Head of the Mossad was lit up. "You're all I needed," he said, and grabbed the son of the Head of the Mossad by his shirt. "You're all I needed," he said again and pulled a flick knife out of his pocket. It went click and the blade sprang out. And the son of the Head of the Mossad closed his eyes and swayed on his long legs. Simon was so glad to see the son of the Head of the Mossad frightened, that he didn't feel sick any more. Dozens of ideas raced through his head, about how to humiliate the son of the Head of the Mossad. "You know," he lied to the son of the Head of the Mossad, "Gabi always gets a kick out of telling people what a small dick you've got. How about pulling them down so I can see for myself." And after he made him take off his trousers and underpants, Simon took away his shirt too. Then he went home, and the following day he woke up with a terrible headache. The son of the Head of the Mossad had to stagger home on his stilts, only to discover, when he finally got there and opened the door, that his father was standing in the hallway staring at him, dumbfounded. His dad demanded an immediate account of everything that had happened. And he told him about the blade, and about Simon. His dad asked if Simon had actually touched him at any point, and whether he had tried to stand his ground, and whether Ehud had stripped too, because the son of the Head of the Mossad forgot to tell him that Ehud had stayed behind on the court to keep practising. When he'd finished the interrogation, the Head of the Mossad said: "OK, you can go and get dressed," and he sat down at his desk, fuming.

The son of the Head of the Mossad got into bed naked, pulled the blanket over his head, and started to cry. His mother, who had just stood there the whole time his father was interrogating him and hadn't said a word, came in and hugged him till he stopped crying, and she thought he was asleep. After that, for the first time in his life, he heard his father yelling in the living room. Only some of the words reached him through the blanket, like "your fault", "not even a scratch," "no - I'm not overreacting", and "Ehud, for one".

The next morning, the Head of the Mossad checked the clip, and put the gun back in the drawer. Then he gave his son a ride to school. They didn't say a word the whole way, as usual. At two o'clock, the son of the Head of the Mossad finished lunch and said he was going out to play basketball.

That night, when the son of the Head of the Mossad came home, he gave his father and mother a tired smile and said, "What a day I had, don't ask." And they didn't. Later, when his father went to the bathroom and his mother was already asleep, he put the gun back in the bottom drawer. Even if they asked him, he wouldn't have answered anyway.

PIPES

When I got to seventh grade, they had a psychologist come to school and put us through a bunch of adjustment tests. He showed me twenty different flash cards, one by one, and asked me what was wrong with the pictures. They all seemed fine to me, but he insisted and showed me the first picture again - the one with the kid in it. "What's wrong with this picture?" he asked in a tired voice. I told him the picture seemed fine. He got really mad and said, "Can't you see the boy in the picture doesn't have any ears?" The truth is that when I looked at the picture again, I did see that the kid had no ears. But the picture still seemed fine to me. The psychologist classed me as "suffering from severe perceptual disorders", and had me transferred to carpentry school. When I got there, it turned out I was allergic to sawdust, so they transferred me to metalworking class. I was pretty good at it, but I didn't really enjoy it. To tell

the truth, I didn't really enjoy anything in particular.
When I finished school, I started working in a factory
that made pipes. My boss was an engineer with a
diploma from a top technical college. A brilliant
guy. If you showed him a picture of a kid without
ears or something like that, he'd work it out in no
time.

After work I'd stay on at the factory and make
myself odd-shaped pipes, winding ones that looked
like curled-up snakes, and I'd roll marbles through
them. I know it sounds like an idiotic thing to do,
and I didn't even enjoy it, but I went on doing it
anyway.

One night I made a pipe that was really com-
plicated, with lots of twists and turns in it, and
when I rolled a marble in, it didn't come out at the
other end. At first I thought it was just stuck in
the middle, but after I tried it with about twenty
more marbles, I realised they were simply disap-
pearing. I know that everything I say sounds kind
of stupid. I mean everyone knows that marbles
don't just disappear, but when I saw the marbles
go in at one end of the pipe and not come out at
the other end, it didn't even strike me as strange.
It seemed perfectly okay actually. That was when I
decided to make myself a bigger pipe, in the same
shape, and to crawl into it until I disappeared.
When the idea came to me, I was so happy that I
started laughing out loud. I think it was the first

time in my entire life that I laughed.

From that day on, I worked on my giant pipe.
Every evening I'd work on it, and in the morning
I'd hide the parts in the storeroom. It took me
twenty days to finish making it. On the last night
it took me five hours to assemble it, and it took up
about half the shop floor.

When I saw it all in one piece, waiting for me, I
remembered my social studies teacher who said
once that the first human being to use a club wasn't
the strongest person in his tribe or the smartest.
It's just that the others didn't need a club, while
he did. He needed a club more than anyone, to
survive and to make up for being weak. I don't
think there was another human being in the
whole world who wanted to disappear more than I
did, and that's why it was me that invented the
pipe. Me, and not that brilliant engineer with his
technical college degree who runs the factory.

I started crawling inside the pipe, with no idea
about what to expect at the other end. Maybe
there would be kids there without ears, sitting on
mounds of marbles. Could be. I don't know exactly
what happened after I passed a certain point in
the pipe. All I know is that I'm here.

I think I'm an angel now. I mean, I've got
wings, and this circle over my head and there are
hundreds more here like me. When I got here
they were sitting around playing with the marbles

I'd rolled through the pipe a few weeks earlier.

I always used to think that heaven is a place for people who've spent their whole life being good, but it isn't. God is too merciful and kind to make a decision like that. Heaven is simply a place for people who were genuinely unable to be happy on earth. They told me here that people who kill themselves return to live their life all over again, because the fact that they didn't like it the first time doesn't mean they won't fit in the second time. But the ones who really don't fit in the world wind up here. They each have their own way of getting to heaven.

There are pilots who got here by performing a loop at one precise point in the Bermuda Triangle. There are housewives who went through the back of their kitchen cabinets to get here, and mathematicians who found topological distortions in space and had to squeeze through them to get here. So if you're really unhappy down there, and if all kinds of people are telling you that you're suffering from severe perceptual disorders, look for your own way of getting here, and when you find it, could you please bring some cards, because we're getting pretty tired of the marbles.

SHOES

On Holocaust Memorial Day our teacher Sara took us on the 57 bus to visit the Museum of Volhynia Jewry, and I felt very important. All the kids in the class except me, my cousin, and another boy, Druckman, were of Iraqi origin. I was the only one with a grandfather who had died in the Holocaust. The Volhynia House was very beautiful and posh, all made of black marble, like millionaires' houses. It was full of sad black-and-white pictures and lists of people and countries and dead folk. We walked past the pictures in pairs and the teacher said, "Don't touch!" But I did touch one picture, made of cardboard, showing a thin pale man who was crying and holding a sandwich in his hand. The tears came streaming down his cheeks like the lines you see on the street, and my partner, Orit Salem, said she would tell the teacher that I touched it, and I said I didn't care, she could tell whoever she wanted, even the head.

I didn't give a damn. It's my Grandpa and I'm touching whatever I want.

After the pictures they led us into a big hall and showed us a movie about little children who were shoved into a truck and then suffocated by gas. Then an old skinny man got on the stage and told us what bastards and murderers the Nazis were and how he took revenge on them, and even strangled a soldier with his own hands until he died. Jerby, who was sitting next to me, said the old man was lying; the way he looks, there's no way he can make any soldier bite the dust. But I looked the old man in the eye and believed him. He had so much anger in his eyes, that all the violent rage of iron-pumping hoods I've seen seemed like small change in comparison.

Finally, when he finished telling us what he had done during the Holocaust, the old man said that what we had just heard was relevant not only to the past but also for what goes on now, because the Germans still exist and still have a state. He said he was never going to forgive them, and that he hoped we, too, would never ever go visit their country. Because when he went with his parents to Germany fifty years ago everything looked nice, but it ended in hell. People have short memories, he said, especially when bad things are concerned. People tend to forget, he said, but you won't forget. Every time you see a German, you'll remember what I told you. Every time you see German products, be it television (since most televisions here are made by German manufacturers) or anything else, you'll always remember that underneath the elegant wrapping are hidden parts and tubes made of bones and skin and flesh of dead Jews.

On the way out Jerby again said that he'd bet anything the old man never strangled anybody in his life, and I thought to myself it was a good job that at home we had an Amkor refrigerator. Who needs trouble?

Two weeks later my parents came back from a trip abroad and brought me trainers. My older brother had secretly told my mum that that's what I wanted and she got me the best pair in the world. Mum smiled when she gave me the present. She was sure I had no idea what was inside. But I immediately recognised the Adidas logo on the bag. I took out the shoebox and said thank you. The box was rectangular, like a coffin, and inside lay two white shoes with three blue stripes and the inscription "Adidas" on their side; I didn't have to open the box to know what they looked like.

"Let's put them on," my mother said and took out the wrapping paper, "to make sure they fit." She was smiling all the time, and had no idea what was going on.

"They're from Germany, you know," I told her, squeezing her hand tightly.

"Of course, I know," Mum smiled, "Adidas is the best brand in the world."

"Grandpa was from Germany, too," I tried to give her a hint.

"Grandpa was from Poland," Mum corrected me. For a moment she became sad, but soon recovered. She put one shoe on my foot and started to tie the laces. I kept quiet. I realised there was nothing doing. Mum didn't have a clue. She had never been to Volhynia House. Nobody ever explained it to her. For her, shoes were just shoes and Germany was Poland. I let her put the shoes on me and kept silent. There was no point in telling her and making her even sadder.

I thanked her again and kissed her on the cheek and said I was going to play football.

"You will be careful, eh?" my Dad called, laughing from his armchair in the front room. "Don't wear out the soles right away." I looked again at the pale hide covering my feet. I looked at them and remembered everything the old man who had strangled said we should remember. I touched the blue stripes of the Adidas and remembered my cardboard grandfather.

"Are the shoes comfortable?" my mother asked.

"Sure they're comfortable," my brother answered for me. "These are not cheap Israeli trainers. These are the same trainers that the great Cruyff wears." I tiptoed slowly towards the door, trying to put as little weight as I could on the shoes. And so I made my way gingerly to Monkeys Park. Outside the kids from Borochov Monkeys neighbourhood had formed three teams: Holland, Argentina and Brazil. It so happened that Holland needed a player, so they agreed to let me join, although they never accept anyone who's not from Borochov.

At the beginning of the game I still remembered not to kick with the tip of my shoe, so as not to hurt Grandpa, but after a while I forgot, just as the old man at Volhynia House said people tend to do, and I even managed to kick a match-winning goal. But when the game was over I remembered and looked at the shoes. All of a sudden they became so comfortable, much bouncier than when they were in the box. "Some goal, eh?" I reminded Grandpa on the way home, "the goalie didn't know what hit him." Grandpa said nothing, but judging by the tread I could tell that he, too, was pleased.

SHOOTING CLINT

I got Clint for my ninth birthday from Sammy Zagoori who was probably the cheapest kid in the whole class. He ran out of luck, and his dog had puppies right on the day of my party. There were four of them, and his uncle was going to dump them all in the river, so Sammy, who only cared about how not to spend anything on the class gift, took one of them and gave it to me. The puppy was tiny, with a bark that sounded more like a wheeze, and when he got mad, he'd give a deep, low kind of growl that didn't sound anything like a puppy. He seemed to think he was really tough, so I called him Clint.

From Day One, my Dad couldn't stand the sight of him. Clint didn't care much for Dad either. The truth is Clint didn't like anyone much, except me. From the start, even when he was just a little puppy, he'd bark at everyone. And when he grew a little bigger, he would snap at anyone who came too close. Even Mickey, who isn't the kind of guy that says things about people, said that my dog was messed up. He never snapped or did anything bad to me though. He'd just keep jumping on me and licking me, and whenever I'd move away from him he'd start whining. Mickey said it didn't mean anything, because I was the one who fed him. But I know lots of dogs who bark even at the people who feed them, and I knew that what Clint and I had going for us wasn't about food, and that he really did like me. He just did. He didn't need a reason. Who knows what a dog thinks? But it was something strong. Fact is, my sister fed him too, but he hated her like hell.

In the morning, when I'd go to school, he'd want to come with me, but I'd make him stay behind because I was afraid he'd make a racket. We had a fence around our garden. And sometimes, when I'd come home, I'd still catch Clint barking at some poor slob who dared to walk down our street. He'd get so mad that he'd smash right into the fence. But the second he spotted me, he'd just melt. Right away, he'd start crawling on the ground, wagging his tail and barking about all the creeps who'd got on his nerves that day by walking down our street, and about how they'd barely made it out of there alive. He'd already bitten a couple of them, but lucky for me they were kids so they didn't complain, because even without that kind of thing, my Dad was on Clint's case, just waiting for the chance to get rid of him.

Finally it happened. Clint bit my sister, and they had to take her to hospital for stitches. Soon as they got home, Dad took Clint to the car. I didn't need long to figure out what was going to happen, and I started crying, so Mum told Dad: "Come on Joshua, why don't you just forget it. It's the kid's dog. Just look at how upset he is."

Dad didn't say anything, just told my big brother to come with him. "I need him too," Mum tried. "He's a watchdog, against thieves."

And my dad stopped short just before he got into the car, and said: "What do you need a watchdog for? Nobody's ever tried to steal anything in this neighborhood. What's to steal here anyway?" They dumped Clint in the river, and stuck around to watch him being washed away. I know, because my big brother told me so. I didn't talk to anyone about it though, and except for the night they took him away, I didn't even cry at all.

Three days later, Clint turned up at school. I heard him barking from below. He was awfully dirty, and smelly too, but other than that he was just the same. I was proud of him for coming back. It proved that everything Mickey had said about his not really loving me wasn't true. Because if the thing between Clint and me had been just about food he wouldn't have come right back to me. It was smart of him to come straight to school too. Because if he'd headed straight home without me, I don't know what my Dad would've done. Even so, soon as we got to the house, Dad wanted me to get rid of him. But Mum told him that maybe Clint had learned his lesson, and that maybe he'd behave himself now. So I hosed him down in the garden, and Dad said that from now on he'd be on a leash all the time, and that if he pulled anything again, that would be it.

Truth is, Clint didn't learn a thing from what happened. He just got a little crazier. And every day, when I'd get home from school, I'd see him barking like a maniac at anyone who happened to walk by. One day, I came home and he wasn't there. Dad wasn't there either. Mum said they'd come from the Border Patrol because they'd heard he was such a smart animal they wanted to recruit him, and that now Clint would be a scout-dog who'd track down terrorists that tried to sneak across the border. I pretended to believe her. That evening, when Dad came back with the car, Mum whispered something in his ear, and he shook his head. He'd driven fifty miles this time, all the way across the bay, before setting Clint loose, just to make sure he wouldn't be able to come back. I know, because my big brother told me so. My brother also said it was because Clint had got loose that afternoon, and had managed to bite the dog-catcher too. I wasn't mad at Mum for lying. I knew she was doing it for my sake.

Fifty miles is a long way, even by car, and on foot it's a thousand times more, especially for a dog. I mean a dog's step is like a quarter of a human's. But three weeks later, Clint was back. He was there waiting for me at the school gate. Didn't even bark, he was so exhausted. Just wagged his tail without getting up. I brought him some water, and he must have lapped up about ten bowls of it. When Dad saw him, he was speechless. That dog's like a curse," he told Mum, who quickly got Clint some bones from the kitchen. That evening I let him sleep in my bed. He fell asleep before me, and all night long he just whined and growled, snapping at anyone who pissed him off in his dream.

In the end it was Grandma of all people that he had to pick on. He didn't even bite her. Just jumped on her, and knocked her over. She got a nasty bump on her head. Everyone helped her up. Me too. But then Mum sent me to the kitchen for a glass of water, and by the time I got back I saw Dad dragging Clint towards the car looking really mad. I didn't even try, and neither did Mum. We knew he had it coming. Dad asked my brother to come along again, except that this time he told him to bring his M16. My brother was just an army cook, but he had a gun anyway. At first, he didn't catch on, and asked Dad what he needed a gun for. And Dad said it was to make Clint stop coming back.

They took him to the dump, and shot him in the head. My brother told me so. Clint didn't realise what was going to happen. He'd been in a good mood, and was turned on by all the rubbish he found at the dump. And then, bang! From the second my brother told me about it, I hardly thought about Clint at all. All those other times, I used to wonder about him a lot, trying to guess where he was and what he was doing. But this time, there was nothing to wonder about any more, so I tried to think about him as little as possible.

Six months later he came back. He was waiting for me in the school yard. There was something wrong with one of his legs, one of his eyes was closed, and his jaw looked completely paralysed. But soon as he saw me, he seemed really happy, like nothing had ever happened. When I got him home, Dad wasn't back from work yet, and Mum wasn't there either. But even when they did come home, they didn't say a thing. And that was it. Clint stayed from then on. Twelve more years. Eventually he died of old age. And he never bit anyone again. Every now and then, when someone would pass by our fence on a bike or just make some noise, you could still see him get worked up and try to pounce, but somehow he always ran out of steam in the middle.

SURPRISE EGG

*T*o *Danny, with love*

This is a true story. Three months ago a woman
about thirty-two years old met her death in a suicide bomb attack near a bus-stop. She wasn't the
only one who met her death, lots of others did too.
But this story is about her.

People who are killed in terrorist attacks are
taken to the Forensic Institute in Abu-Kabir for an
autopsy. Many key figures in Israeli society have
wondered about this procedure, and even the people
who work at Abu-Kabir don't always understand it
exactly. Everyone knows the cause of death in
those attacks, and a body isn't some surprise egg
that you open without knowing what you're going
to find inside – a sailboat maybe, or a racing car or
a plastic koala. Whenever they operate they
always find the same things after all – little pieces
of metal, nails or other kinds of shrapnel. Very few

surprises. But in this case, of the thirty-two-year-old woman, they did find something else. Inside her body, besides all those pieces of metal that had torn into her flesh, this woman had dozens of tumours, really big ones. There were tumours in her stomach, in her liver and in her intestines, but especially in her head. When the pathologist peeked into her skull, the first thing he said was "Oh my God" because it was simply frightening. He saw dozens of tumours that had inched their way into her brain like a swarm of cruel ants that just wanted to devour more and more.

And this is where the scientific observation comes in: if this woman hadn't died in a terrorist attack, she would have collapsed within a week and would have died from her tumours within a month, two months tops. It's hard to see how a young woman like that could have been suffering from such an advanced cancer without its being diagnosed at all. Maybe she was one of those people who don't like medical examinations or maybe she figured the pain and the dizziness she'd been having were something routine that would just go away. In any case, when her husband arrived to identify her at the morgue, the pathologist had a hard time deciding whether to tell him about it or not. On the one hand, it was a revelation that could have offered some comfort – there's no point in tormenting yourself with thoughts like "if only she hadn't gone to work that day" or "if only I'd driven her" when you know that your wife was about to die anyway. On the other hand, this news could make the grief even more distressing and turn her arbitrary and horrible death into something much more horrible: a death experienced twice over in a sense, making it inevitable, as if someone up there wanted to make absolutely sure, and no "what ifs" could have saved her, not even hypothetically. Then again, the pathologist thought to himself, what difference does it really make? The woman's dead, her husband's a widower, her children are orphans, that's what matters, that's what's sad, and all the rest is nonsense.

The husband asked to identify his wife by her foot. Most people identify their loved ones by their faces. But he asked to identify her by her foot, because he thought that if he saw her dead face, the sight would haunt him his whole life, or rather, what remained of it. He had loved her and he knew her so well that he could identify her by each and every part of her body, and somehow her foot seemed the most remote, neutral and far-removed. He looked at the foot for another few seconds, even after he'd identified the barely visible wavy contours of her toenails, the slightly crooked, chubby big toe, the perfect arching of her sole. Maybe it was a bad idea, he thought to himself as he continued to look at the little foot (size 6), maybe it was a bad idea to choose the foot. A dead person's face looks like a sleeping person's but with a dead person's foot there's no mistaking the death lurking under every toenail. "That's her," he told the pathologist after a while, and left the room.

Among the people at the woman's funeral was the pathologist. He wasn't the only one, the mayor of Jerusalem was there, and the minister of internal security. Both of them made personal promises to the husband, repeating his first name and the deceased woman's name many times as they spoke, to avenge her cruel death. They gave a dramatic and vivid description of how they would hunt down those responsible for dispatching the murderer (there was no way of taking revenge on the suicide bomber himself.) The husband looked rather uneasy with all those promises. It seemed that he wasn't all that interested, and the only reason he was trying to hide it was to avoid hurting the feelings of all those impassioned public figures who were naïve enough to believe that their vehement speeches could offer him some solace.

The funeral was the second time the pathologist had considered the idea of telling the husband that his wife had been on the verge of death in any case, to offset some of the uneasiness and vengefulness in the air, but this time too he kept it to himself. On his way back, he tried to think philosophically about everything that had happened.

What is cancer, he thought to himself, if not a terrorist attack from above? What is it that God is doing if not terrorising us in protest against ... something. Something so lofty and transcendental that it is beyond our grasp? Like most of his work at the institute, this thought too was surgically precise, but it didn't really make any difference.

The night after the funeral, the husband had a sad dream in which the dead foot was rubbing against his face, a dream which caused him to wake up in a state of fright and agitation. He tiptoed into the kitchen, so as not to wake the children, and made himself a cup of tea without turning on the light. Even after he'd finished drinking the steaming tea, he went on sitting in the dark kitchen. He tried to think of something he would like to do, something that would make him happy, anything. Even things he couldn't really allow himself because of the kids or because he couldn't afford to, but nothing came to mind. He felt full of a dense and sour substance that was blocking his chest, and it wasn't grief. It was something much more serious than grief. After all those years, life now seemed like no more than a trap, a maze, not even a maze, just a room that was all walls, no door. "There must be something," he persisted, "something I'd like to happen even if I can't possibly make it, anything."

Some people commit suicide after someone

close to them goes, others turn to religion and there are those who sit in the kitchen all night and don't even wait for the sun to rise. The light from outside was beginning to creep into the apartment and pretty soon the little ones would be waking up. He tried to recall once more the feel of the foot in his dream, and the way it always happens with dreams, all he could do was reconstruct it but not really experience it. "If only she hadn't gone to work that day," he thought, forcing himself to get up, "if only I'd driven her. She'd still be alive now, sitting here in the kitchen with me."

My Brother's Depressed

It isn't like just anyone walked up to you in the street and told you he's depressed. It's my brother, and he wants to kill himself. And of all the people in the world, he had to tell it to me. Because I'm the person he loves the most, and I love him too, I really do, but that's a biggie. I mean like wow.

Me and my little brother are standing there together in the Shenkin playground, and my dog Hendrix, is tugging away at the leash, trying to bite this little kid in overalls in the face. And me, I'm fighting with Hendrix with one hand, and searching my pockets for a lighter with the other. "Don't do it," I tell my brother. The lighter isn't there, in either pocket. "Why not?" my little brother asks. "My girlfriend's left me for a fireman. I hate university. Here's a light. And my parents are the most pitiful people in the world." He throws me his Cricket lighter. I catch it. Hendrix runs away. He pounces on the kid in the overalls, pushes him flat on the lawn and his scary Rottweiler jaw clamps down on the kid's face. Me and my brother try to pry Hendrix off the kid, but he won't budge. The overalls' mother screams. The kid himself is suspiciously subdued. I kick Hendrix as hard as I can, but he couldn't care less. My brother finds a metal bar on the lawn, and whams it down on the dog's head. There's a sickening sound of something cracking, and Hendrix collapses. The mother is screaming. Hendrix has bitten off her kid's nose, but completely. And now Hendrix is dead. My brother killed him. And besides, he wants to kill himself too. Because to him having his girlfriend double-cross him with a fireman seems like the most humiliating thing in the world. I think a fire-man is pretty impressive actually, rescuing people and all that. But as far as he's concerned she could just as well fuck a refuse lorry. Now the kid's mother is attacking me. She's trying to gouge out my eyes with her long fingernails that are painted with repulsive white polish. My brother picks up the metal bar and bangs her one on the head too. He's allowed, he's depressed.

VACUUM SEAL

The sergeant took Alon's vacuum-sealed bandage and pushed it into the pail. Air bubbles rose to the surface. The sergeant ignored them and went on pressing the bandage down to the bottom, smirking. Alon couldn't help feeling that the sergeant was trying to drown his bandage, his personal bandage, for no reason whatsoever.

The flow of bubbles stopped. The sergeant took his hand out of the pail and gave the wet corpse a look of contempt. "Is this what you call a vacuum seal, Schreiber? There's a hole in this seal as big as a cunt." The sergeant moved closer, till their faces were practically touching, and said in a loud whisper: "I bet you never once saw a girl's cunt, did you, Schreiber?"

Alon had once seen a girl's cunt. He'd seen it many times, except he couldn't see what her loving, naked body had to do with that word.

"I asked you a question, Schreiber." Alon felt

as if the sergeant had invaded his brain and was undressing her against her will, against his will. He wouldn't let him destroy that too. He wouldn't.

"I can't hear you, Schreiber."

"No, Sir."

"Never mind, it isn't your fault you were born a loser. Why don't you ask your mother nicely? maybe she'll show you the hole you came out of. Lugassi, I wouldn't be laughing if I had a face like yours."

The sergeant turned towards Alon. There was a menacing look in his eyes. "Am I imagining things, Schreiber, or are you really crying?"

"No, Sir."

"Schreiber, you're a poor excuse for a human being, a poor excuse for a soldier, and a poor excuse for a vacuum sealer." The sergeant was screaming by then, spraying droplets of spit in Alon's face. The droplets burned as they hit his skin. It felt like acid, an acid that consumes everything. "I can't make a man out of you. Even God Almighty couldn't do that. But I can make a soldier out of you. Tomorrow morning, I expect to see every single one of your underpants and vests vacuum sealed. One by one. And they'd better be done properly this time. And y'know why, Schreiber?" The sergeant's voice rose even higher. "Because good vacuum sealing is an inseparable part of being a good soldier. I bet you're smiling,

Bugamilsky." The sergeant turned to face Bugamilsky with a nervous jerk, "It'd take a rookie retard like you to smile when I'm explaining about vacuum sealing. I'd like to see you smile after you cross the Zaharani with your trousers full of Arab shit and crud. And then, when you want to change into a pair of dry trousers and some clean, dry underpants ..." The sergeant moved over towards Bugamilsky's bed, opened the rucksack and registered a look of mock surprise. "You'll discover it's on account of your lousy vacuum seal that they're sopping wet too. I bet you'll be laughing then too, you dickhead, when you try to keep going with a ton of crud in your underpants, like some baby that made in his trousers."

"Bugamilsky didn't take his vacuum sealing seriously, which is why he's going to do two extra hours of guard duty tonight. Private, write that down. Anyone else here too smart to bother with vacuum sealing?" The sergeant scanned the platoon.

Alon did take it seriously. Vacuum sealing was his only chance.

That night, Alon vacuum sealed his clothes. He could tell he was getting more and more skilful with each item, and he couldn't help feeling proud of himself as he studied his last vacuum-sealed vest. He was ready.

He closed his eyes softly and started vacuum sealing himself.

During roll-call, the sergeant was more short-tempered than ever, coming down on everybody. When he got to Alon, he grabbed him by his shirt, leaned over and shouted the same sentence in his ear over and over again. Alon listened to the droplets of spit shattering against the vacuum seal. Their frenzied rhythm reminded him of raindrops banging helplessly against a taut plastic awning. Not a single droplet hit him.

After nightfall, he had to crawl for fifty minutes, shouting "I'm a snake, I'm a liar," because he'd declared that his weapon was clean, and the sergeant had found some oil in the assembly.

When Alon rose to his feet, he was pleased to discover that he didn't have even one drop of dirt on him. The vacuum seal had done its job.

At one point, he thought the seal wasn't airtight. It was his Saturday off, two weeks before the end of basic training. She said the army had changed him, had made him different, that he was recoiling from her kisses, avoiding her touch. How could he tell her about the synthetic taste in his mouth, the artificial, sticky touch of her body, the suffocating feeling? For a moment he thought he'd heard the sound of air rushing through some hidden hole in the transparent seal. But it was just the murmur of the door closing behind her. He wanted to cry, but there were no tears in his eyes. What's the point of a transparent vacuum seal when you're wet on the inside anyway?

He looked at himself in the mirror, at his shiny identity tag, at his neatly starched service dress, at the razor in his right hand. He drew the razor closer to the clearly visible artery in his neck. "Basic training is over," he whispered. "Time to undo the seal."

SHOSHI

It was so easy to get him to start talking. And once he started, you just couldn't shut him up. The shooting went on and on, and I began to think the militants weren't attacking us out of some foggy fundamentalist motivation, but simply out of a deep-seated urge to get Shoshi to clam up. Shoshi told us that the Syrians teach the Hizbollah to shoot at our radio antennas because that's where the officers always are. He swore on the life of his grandfather (who had died in Gdańsk in '42) that there used to be a type of rabbit with tails that looked exactly like antennas and that the irresponsible combat technique of the Hizbollah had practically wiped them out. "I read about it in the *Farmer's Almanac*," Shoshi added quickly to dispel any doubts we might have. There was no sign of the shooting letting up. Tziyyon lay in the corner, his hands over his ears. "I think he listens to his Walkman during the battle, Sir, and his shirt isn't tucked in either. You could bring him up on charges for that, Sir," Shoshi said in a sombre voice.

"Shut up, Shoshi, I'm trying to think."

"Sir, I have a wonderful idea for raising morale in the unit," Shoshi ignored my request.

"Quiet, please. Quiet. I can't take it anymore?" Tziyyon begged, half to Shoshi, half to the Hizbollah.

"... why don't we play take-offs? Who'd like to begin?" Shoshi was at it in his didactic voice.
Meir the Bukharan, who had lost a lot of blood, started to shiver and we didn't even have a first-aid kit.

Shoshi began screaming hysterically. "A blender. Bukhara is doing a take-off of a blender."

Tziyyon leapt up at Shoshi and slapped him hard.

"As if it's not bad enough that we're stuck in enemy territory without so much as a radio or a bandage, and Meir dying right in our hands, we have to listen to your crap and all your crazy lies about frigging rabbits ..."

"Lies? Who are you calling a liar?" Shoshi whispered indignantly. "Just for your information, Tziyyon, I could save every last one of you: you and Zohar and Blender. But just because of this..." he brandished an accusatory finger in his face, "just because of this, I'm going to let you die."

Outside, the shooting continued and I began wondering why the Hizbollah didn't come up to where we were and throw in a grenade. We hadn't fired a single shot in twenty minutes. As if he'd read my thoughts, Tziyyon changed clips, switched from automatic and fired a single bullet at Shoshi, right between the eyes. "Are you crazy? You killed him." I screamed in horror.

"Look what you've done, you maniac," Shoshi screamed back. Apparently he was prepared to die, but categorically unwilling to clam up.

I looked at Shoshi's bloody face. "It's like a bad dream," I whispered.

"It's like a bad dream," Shoshi mimicked my voice. "What do you think, that you're going to wake up back in the tent and discover you've wet your bedroll? The sonovabitch killed me." There was no doubt about that. The bullet had smashed his skull, and we all knew perfectly well that no human being could possibly stay alive after taking something like that. "Just you wait, you piece of shit. My cousin's a lieutenant colonel in the Judge Advocate General's office. I'll make sure they show your mother bawling on the evening news after they sentence you to life," Shoshi sobbed, and curled up in the corner, finally beginning to behave like a dead guy. Tziyyon was on the verge of losing it. I knew we'd have to surrender. I went outside, waving the bloodstained white vest I'd taken off of Meir, who continued to shiver. Tziyyon followed me, slightly stooped, his eyes glazed over.

I couldn't see anyone at first, just their radio antenna behind a sand dune. But in no time at all I discovered it wasn't a radio at all. Coming out from behind the heap of sand was a rabbit with a tail that looked like an antenna, a smoking Kalashnikov in his hands. "We blew it, guys, they're Israeli," he shouted. Three other rabbits emerged from the dunes, jumped onto the jeep and drove off.

"I don't believe it," Tziyyon whispered, "a talking rabbit."

We returned to the hideaway, and Tziyyon gave Shoshi a gentle shove. "Shoshi, I'm really sorry for calling you a liar. There really are rabbits like that. And also for killing you."

"Forget it," said Shoshi. "We were all uptight."

Meir continued to shiver.

Shoshi 2

Tziyyon's getting out in two weeks. He's invited all of us to a party at his place on the kibbutz. Shoshi said I ought to come up with some excuse not to go. "Those kibbutzniks are all cannibals," Shoshi was at it again. "They eat each other alive over there, like there's no tomorrow. If they weren't all so discreet, everyone would know about it by now. Someone just has to get drunk, to confuse you with the work manager and to figure it's your fault he got the late shift - and wham, you'll wind up in the digestive tract of some fat-cat Marxist creep." Ever since the incident in Lebanon he's been totally unbearable. Especially the business with the letter to the battalion commander.

In the first few weeks after the incident in Lebanon, he'd wander around camp, sticking a finger into the hole in his head, then pulling it out again, and shouting: "I'm dead, wow ... I'm dead." Shlomo the cook fainted at the sight of him, and later he handed the company commander a transfer form where he'd written that he wasn't prepared to serve in the same unit as a corpse because it's against his religion. Once Akiva got Shoshi to calm down and stop his nonsense, Shoshi handed the battalion commander an official Application for Recognition as a Fallen Soldier, which would exempt him from guard duty. The battalion commander, Maksim, blew a fuse when he saw the application, and filed an unfit conduct complaint against Shoshi. At the hearing, he sentenced Shoshi to fourteen days in solitary. Shoshi threw a fit: "You have no idea who you're fooling with. The writer's a friend of mine. You're going to pay for this," he screamed. Yonni the NCO and I had to drag him out of the room. Maksim the battalion commander asked me to report anything unusual that Shoshi did. Two days after they let him out of prison, Shoshi smeared peanut butter all over the patrol jeep. He said it would confuse the enemy's camels. I didn't mention it to Maksim. Why go looking for trouble. Shoshi is capable of having my name misspelled too.

Today he told me sadly that he'd sent a black wreath to Meir the Bukharan's parents on behalf of the unit. "I miss him so," he whispered, wiping a tear from the corner of his eye. "But Meir isn't dead," I reminded him. "He's just been reassigned. He works in a canteen now, that's what he does."

Shoshi was inconsolable. "Stop blubbering. Meir's alive," I said, shaking him by the shoulders.

"So he's alive, so he's alive, so what?" Shoshi protested furiously. "It would have been much nicer if he'd died in Lebanon. "A canteen," he hissed in disgust. "Those Bukharans haven't got a drop of aesthetic sensibility. You should've choked him before the APC came to pick us up."

"Shoshi - what's that stand for?" I tried to steer the conversation onto a new track. "It's short for Shoshana. My parents always wanted a daughter," Shoshi came round. He closed his eyes and wiggled his arse, and I could tell he was about to start singing. He does that sometimes. You can just tell he watches lots of Bollywood movies. "When I was a tot / Father beat me a lot / He didn't want a son / But what's done is done."

His songs last over an hour, and he does this dance in the middle. I couldn't take it any more. I went to see Akiva about getting a transfer. That's when he showed me a write-up in the paper, about Tziyyon. Tziyyon has been declared missing. "Vanished, like the earth swallowed him," Akiva whispered, and gave me a meaningful wink. I went back to the tent, got into bed without undressing and didn't even take off my shoes. I pulled the covers all the way up and shut my eyes and tried to fall asleep.

Tonight I'm going to have another dream about

how Shoshi enlists in the Foreign Legion and all
the Algerians convert and move to Israel. It's
always like that.

SHOSHI 3

At his discharge party, we bought Shoshi this book, *Gaza Blues,* by Samir El-youssef and Etgar Keret, and gave it to him as a present. "It's a shitty book," Shoshi scowled. "Except for two ... sorry, three stories, it's all crap. Any idiot can put out a book these days, in some two-bit press, and blow a fortune on it, all because of some infantile delusion that sooner or later it'll earn him a fuck." Truth is Shoshi had a point, and the only reason Akiva had bought the book was that it was on sale. "Know what, Zohar? I know this Etgar guy personally. What a pussy. Whatever I tell him to do, he does. Wanna see?"

"Forget it, Shoshi, let's just have some cake, and split. It's really late." I begged.

"Shit, Zohar, it's my party. Lemme enjoy it. Just watch me skewer him." Shoshi started walking on the ceiling, and interrupting the unity of plot and time with all kinds of nasty schemes.

"Come on, Shoshi, quit it," I insisted. It's going to wind up costing us two zloty." Shoshi just went on and on, deliberately destroying the coherence of the plot.

"Don't worry, Zohar, that Etgar is such a wimp. We go a long way back, he wouldn't dare interrupt our

Samir El-youssef

For Judith and John, my family

THE DAY THE BEAST GOT THIRSTY

I liked listening to Ahmad.

I liked listening to Ahmad especially after I had a couple of joints. But sometimes Ahmad used to say things that made me realise that unless I leave the country I shall go mad.

Take, for example, that day when he was telling me how bad things were getting. He was absolutely sure that a total war was imminent in the region. But when he saw the effect on me of what he was saying, he hastened to announce that after that inevitable war everything was going to be all right.

"Wait until this war is over and done with, and soon after everything will be all right," he said, trying to comfort me.

"But how soon will that be?" I asked, getting no less worried.

"I should not think more than twenty, perhaps, thirty years!" he replied calmly and confidently.

"Thirty years?" I exclaimed.

"Maximum!" he replied, trying to re-assure me.

It was then that I realised that unless I left the country I was going to go mad. But in truth, I had been trying to get away even before Ahmad had told me about that imminent and inescapable thirty years war. I had tried to obtain a visa to Germany through the help of a wise travel agent, but to no avail.

II

"With this sort of a travel document, it is impossible for you to enter Germany," the travel agent declared in an unmistakably authoritative voice. Yet he assured me, with the same authoritative voice, that he was willing to get me a visa for the sum of fifty thousand liras. I felt he was a crook, nevertheless I handed him my travel document and gave him the money. I wanted to question his promise, but I did not have the courage to do so until I saw him tucking my money into the inside pocket of his jacket. I could not help it any more and hurried to ask him how it was possible for him to get me a visa to Germany, if my passport was not valid there. He knew exactly what I was getting at, and he could not ignore it.

Staring at me silently, but with the look of

someone who had been offended, he reached into his pocket, took the bundle of money out, and threw it in front of me on the smooth wooden top of his desk.

"If you do not trust me, you`d better go and look for another travel agency!" he said firmly, stressing the word "agency". He turned his face to one side as if to inform me that nothing I could say would make him accept my case again.

Now I was sure that the man was a crook. But instead of leaving and congratulating myself on a narrow escape from another fixer who sold visas that took you nowhere, I remained sitting, looking apologetic and thinking of a way to smooth things over. I must confess the man's performance had impressed me deeply. He was the sort of performer that I could not resist watching. Besides, he had given me the only sign of hope of getting out of the country that I had ever had. I apologised to him, and mumbled something to the effect that I had only asked an innocent question. I assured him that I did trust him - I trusted him more that I trusted my own family.

Of course he did not believe me, but looked pleased all the same. And with the same authoritative voice, he declared that he had a respectable agency, again stressing the word "agency". He explained that he was not willing to compromise his business or his reputation for the meagre sum which I had given him. He went on, swearing on his father's grave and the life of his wife and children that half of that money was going into the pockets of the staff at the German embassy in Cyprus, and the other half was the mere cost of the journey there. For a few seconds, I felt sorry for him, and practically promised him an equal sum once he had brought me the visa. But, luckily I refrained. I just apologised again for my earlier suspicions.

He looked happier now. And picking up the bundle of money, and putting it back into his pocket - a move that alerted me once again - he told me how many visas he had managed to obtain in the last few years.

"Do you remember such and such a person who used to work in the post office."

I did not remember. In fact I did not know such a person, but nodded all the same.

"He is now in Australia," he said triumphantly. "And do you know so and so who had a stall in the market."

I did not know him either, but nodded again.

"Last year I got him a visa to Austria, and look at him now! Look at his family! I swear by the dearest thing in my life he is sending them no less than a thousand dollars a month!" he said.

I knew he was lying. But I liked listening to liars.

III

Ahmad, however, was not a liar. But sometimes he said things, which could drive you mad.

I really liked listening to him.

And that morning, after I had left the travel agent, I smoked another joint and went to the café hoping to see him. I urgently needed to listen to him, I thought to myself. I was certain that he would come up with something which would reassure me that trusting a crook of a travel agent was a worthwhile risk even for the remote hope of leaving this country.

I was not disappointed.

"The situation is highly suspicious!"

That was the first thing Ahmad said when I saw him in the café.

"What situation do you mean?" I asked foolishly.

"The negotiations between us and the Americans, of course!" he replied.

"Ha!"

"Ha what? We must be careful!" he said urging me. "That bugger Arafat cannot be trusted for a moment. Once the Americans smile at him, he is ready to sell the *intifada*, to sell out everything and rush behind them."

"Is that what you think?" I asked with the

same foolish tone of voice.

"Oh, yes!" he confirmed. "We must keep our eyes open before he fools us and does what the Americans tell him to do."

I promised him to keep an eye on Arafat, but he did not look very impressed by my promise. Like most members of Fatah that I knew, Ahmad never spared an opportunity to swear at Arafat, and accuse him of all sorts of things. But he could never tolerate a word against him from someone who was not a member of Fatah. And I was not a member of Fatah.

"What do you expect from somebody whose uncle was Hajj Amin Al-hussainy?" he told me once, after Arafat had declared that he was willing to give up political violence. "Was not his uncle a traitor? And is it not true what they say that boys take after their uncles?"

We were sitting in the same café that we had frequented since we first met. The owner of the café did not like us, but he ignored us. He did not want any trouble.

"What do you expect after that?" Ahmad asked, rhetorically. He often asked rhetorical questions.

"Hmmm!" I hummed trying to encourage him to keep talking.

"The situation is highly suspicious!" he announced again, and went on telling me all about the play he intended to produce.

"What is it about?" I interrupted, impatiently.

"What is it about?" He repeated my question in astonishment as if he did not expect me, of all people, to ask such a silly question. "It is about our people, of course, our just cause - what else?"

"What! Another play about our cause?" I protested, stressing the words "our cause".

"But this one you will like very much," he replied in an overexcited tone of voice.

I stared at him, waiting to hear the name of the play which I would like very much.

"You will not believe it!" he said, almost choking with that overexcited tone of voice of his.

"I shall believe it."

"Listen to this, then: it is *Om Saad*!" he exclaimed, looking at me in a way as if he was expecting me to start jumping up and down.

"*Om Saad!*"

"Yes!" he affirmed, with a big smile on his face.

"You mean Ghassan Kanafani's novel?"

"Yes! And I know how much you admire Ghassan Kanafani."

"I do admire Ghassan Kanafani, but I do not admire this particular novel of his," I said, stressing the word "admire".

"What?" he protested.

"Yes! It's his worst novel!"

He was surprised and disappointed. And for a moment he looked as if he wanted to say something important, but had changed his mind at the last moment. He waved his arm in a gesture of despair. I felt guilty, and tried to make it up to him.

"The problem is that you are a surrealist!" he said decidedly, as if he was getting himself all ready for a heated debate.

But I was in no mood to get into a debate.

"You must understand," he added, in a paternal tone of voice, "that surrealism is not congenial to this particular era of our cause!"

"Is that what you think?"

"Realism is the style for us!" he said, and paused waiting for my reply.

"But I am not a surrealist," I said, with no great a desire to talk. I was getting bored. "I am a realist, very much so," I added after a while.

"Realist! You, ha!" he protested sarcastically, and shook his head. "What about that story you wrote the other day: a man meets a woman from Mars, he loves her and she loves him, and then she takes him away with her. What sort of a nonsense is this?"

"What's wrong with that?" I said, and started to spin the empty cup of coffee on the saucer.

He was irritated, and muttered something to the effect that I was stoned, and that talking to me was pointless.

He got up suddenly, and left.

IV

I knew he would come back.

He had to come back. He did not have anyone else who would listen to him, talking about his new play, or the cause in general. Whenever he tried to talk to other people about these matters they would either sneak away immediately, or listen for a short while and then ask him: "When are you going to stop talking nonsense?"

I wished he would come back.

I liked listening to Ahmad. He was tolerant with me and generous. He often helped me out when I was in desperate need to buy some cannabis or tablets.

Ahmad was financially comfortable. He received two salaries, one from the Tanzeem and another from the Central Intelligence System. His two brothers in America were also giving him money. He had stayed with his mother after they had left, and they were grateful to him.

Ahmad used to make a lot of money. And he looked after his mother. But the old bag was never happy. She often rowed with him and accused him of being lazy and good-for-nothing. And whenever he came to me and said, "the cause is going through one of its darkest eras," I knew that he must have had a row with his mother, and that the old cow had accused him of being useless.

I felt sorry for him, and once advised him to poison her and do the hell away with her. But he said that he could not do that because he loved her, and could not imagine the world without her, even though she nagged from morning to night.

Ahmad used to make a lot of money.

Two months earlier he had agreed with Abu Shivan, the Leader of the KLP, the Kurdistani Liberation Party, to produce a newsletter on behalf of the party. Abu Shivan had been looking for someone capable of printing a newsletter, and could not find someone more suitable than Ahmad. Of course Ahmad was surprised. True, he was working for the press office of the Tanzeem, and used to produce quite a lot of leaflets, but he had never attempted to produce a Kurdish newsletter. What did he know of the Kurdish language, or even of Kurdistan?

Ahmad was further baffled that Abu Shivan wanted a newsletter when the whole of his KLP numbered no more than seven or eight members. At least that was the number of the men who stayed in the party's base in the Camp.

"It is not for our members in Lebanon," Abu Shivan whispered at Ahmad, so nobody could overhear him, "it is for our members over there!"

"Where, 'over there'?" asked Ahmad, in a whisper, mockingly.

"Kurdistan, of course!"

"And how many comrades do you have, over there, in Kurdistan?" asked Ahmad in the same mockingly whispering voice.

But Abu Shivan did not answer this question. He just gave Ahmad a reproachful look as if to tell him that that was a secret which he could not divulge even to his own mother.

"Ha, ha!" Ahmad hummed, and nodded in a gesture of understanding. However, he was deep down certain that the number of men in Kurdistan was not greater than the number in Lebanon. But what did he care about the number of members of the KLP? For all he cared, there was an opportunity to make some more money, and he was not going to waste it.

Ahmad loved money very much. And some people used to say that he had a half million in the bank. But Ahmad was not certain that Abu Shivan was offering an easy opportunity for making more money. Abu Shivan was a mean bastard, and everybody knew that he hardly ever paid his men their salaries. It was even rumoured that he stole the food supply that his party got from Fatah. Fatah, in those days, used to provide any political party of its allies with money and food supplies. And Abu Shivan nicked the food supply that was supposed to be given to his men. He kept it all to himself, or perhaps sold it in the market, leaving his men in the base with no money or food, cursing the moment that they had to leave the mountains of Kurdistan and come to this God-forsaken country.

Ahmad grew more baffled as to why a mean bastard like Abu Shivan would want to spend a single penny on a newsletter nobody would ever bother to read. He knew from experience that political newsletters and leaflets were rarely read, and at best they were used for no better purpose than to wrap up falafel sandwiches. He often regretted the fact that the masses, as he used to call people, showed no interest in reading such useful publications and knowing the nature of the era which our cause was going through.

"We must print a newsletter at whatever cost!" Abu Shivan exclaimed suddenly, hitting the smooth top of the table with his clenched fist, and adding after a pause, "do you know what Lenin says?"

"What does Lenin say?" Ahmad asked with no great enthusiasm.

"There could be no revolutionary party without a revolutionary newspaper!"

"Ha!" Ahmad replied without getting any more enthusiastic. He was not sure whether Lenin had said such a thing. Nor did he care for what Lenin did or did not say.

In fact Ahmad did not like either Lenin or Karl Marx. They were atheists, and he thought that one should not trust those who did not believe in God.

But that was not the issue then. The important thing for him was that Abu Shivan had made it clear that he was willing to pay any cost in order to have a newsletter.

"Whatever the cost?" Ahmad asked, repeating the same words that Abu Shivan had used. Of course it was these very words that had raised Ahmad's hopes of making some more money.

"Whatever the cost!" Abu Shivan cofirmed.

Wasting no time, Ahmad immediately asked for the sum of forty thousand liras.

"Forty thousand?" cried Abu Shivan in a terrified voice.

Ahmad nodded. Abu Shivan started fumbling in his pockets, producing no more than a few thousand. And he swore that he did not have a penny more, not even to buy petrol for his car. Unflinching, Ahmad, in his turn, kept staring at him as if to make it clear that either he got what he had asked for, or there would be no "revolutionary paper". And soon Abu Shivan realised how serious Ahmad was and reached to his pockets again, this time taking out five thousand from this pocket and five thousand from the next one and so on.

Without bothering to count it, Ahmad rushed to pick up the bundles of money and tuck them into the pockets of his large coat.

Ahmad wore this coat all the time. Wearing it, for him at least, was a sign of his total involvement in his work for the cause. And no small proof was it that the pockets of this coat were stuffed with all sorts of leaflets and scraps of paper. Now, it was stuffed with bundles of money too.

Ahmad loved money very much. He loved to save it, not to spend it. However, he always wore this large old coat, not out of meanness, but because he believed that it was the suitable outfit for someone who was occupied with his work for the sake of the cause, especially at that particular time. The important thing was that he was never mean towards me. He gave me money whenever I was broke. And I often was. I used to spend a lot of money, buying cannabis and tablets. It was very expensive, but I could not possibly live without it.

It was Salim, the Iraqi, who supplied me with these things. He had all sorts of tablets and sometimes he used to display them in front of me, explaining with great enthusiasm the effect of each sort. Salim was also good to me, and often gave me tablets free. But he himself was taking them and he was in need of money most of the time. The salary, which he was getting from the Tanzeem was never enough, especially as the Lebanese currency was in continuous decline. What he used to buy for one thousand in one week, used to cost him two thousand a week later. In order to make up the loss in the value of his salary, Salim had turned to burglary. But he only broke into the houses of his superiors. He considered it a justified sort of burglary.

"Sons of bitches! They receive their budgets in American dollars and pay us in Lebanese money," he told me once after he had broke into the house of Abu Omar, his own superior and friend. And for days Abu Omar and his associates were looking for him, trying to arrest him and recover the video and the television that he had stolen from Abu Omar's house.

V

"Tell your junkie friend that I shall arrest him and put him on a military trial!" Abu Omar told me, two days after the incident.

His associates had captured me in the Camp. They knew that I was a friend of Salim, so they surrounded me and started questioning me as to the whereabouts of Salim. I did not know, but they did not believe me, and dragged me by the sleeves of my shirt to their base where I would be interrogated properly.

"You know more than you are letting on," Abu Omar said in a sober tone of voice. And I thought that such a tone of voice was meant to show that he was an expert in interrogating Mossad agents.

Yes, I knew more than I was letting on, but I was so sleepy that I could hardly hear the question. To Abu Omar's irritation, I actually dozed off.

"He is stoned!" said Abu Omar in an angry voice, and ordered his associates to throw me out: "tell your junkie friend that I am going to arrest him and put him in a military court!"

He carried on shouting while I was being dragged out.

I did not hear of Salim for days, or perhaps for weeks. I was getting more confused, and couldn't be sure. I was taking too many tablets and getting ever more forgetful. And I was so worried that Salim would disappear for good and I would lose my only source of drugs. I went out looking for Ahmad. I thought he could be the only person who would enquire after Salim. I was so worried that Abu Omer and his men had arrested him. I knew what they would do to him - they would not put him on trial, as Abu Omar claimed - they would kill him first and put him on trial afterwards.

"What do you want from that junkie Iraqi?" Ahmad asked, with a look of disgust on his face.

"He is my friend!"

"Friend! And do you think these people know the meaning of friendship?" he went on angrily.

"I tell you the truth! This Revolution has

become so diseased that one could simply despair about the possibility of achieving any sort of victory!" Ahmad cried out.

"Achieving victory!" And do you really hope to achieve any victory? I nearly asked him and laughed, but I was worried that he would be angry and refuse to enquire after Salim.

"While our children are sacrificing their lives in the *intifada*," he went on, "our Revolution is nestling with those scum! Is that right, do you think?"

"Certainly not!" I said, trying, at great pains, to keep a straight face.

"In God's name, they come to us from every corner of the globe. And who do you think is the cause of all this?"

I knew exactly whom he meant, Arafat of course, but did not want to spoil his fun by mentioning the name.

"It is that walking disaster who is sitting in Tunisia, making deals with the Americans now!" he said after a pause.

"Bassem! In the history of our cause," he told me once, "there have been two major disasters: the Catastrophe of '48, and the Walking Disaster!"

Of course I agreed with him, as I always did.

And he went on swearing at Arafat, and didn't stop till he vowed that he would chop his tongue off if Arafat did not sell out and go running after the Americans. I could not help imagining Ahmad doing just that. I thought that after so many years, and after he had realised that Arafat had not sold out, he would put out his tongue and chop it in public to fulfil his vow.

I was wondering what else he could come up with, but he remained silent. He raised his cup of coffee to his lips and sipped noisily. We were sitting in the same café, and the owner looked at us in a way that implied that he wished the earth could open and swallow us up once and for all.

Soon Ahmad relaxed, and went on telling me, with that joyful tone of voice of his, how he was getting on with the play. He said that he had just thought of a wonderful new idea. He thought that he could attach two huge photos on the stage; one, a blown-up photocopy of the Palestinian ID, on the right side of the stage, and another, a blown-up photocopy of the food supply card, on the left.

I thought he had gone absolutely mad.

"But why on each side of the stage? Why not one on top of the other?" I asked foolishly.

"No, that would ruin the symbolic meaning of the play," he replied. "You must see that by attaching such photos, one on each side of the stage, we symbolise our battle between these two realities!"

"Ha, ha!"

"Ha, ha what? Symbolism is the best style for us at this very era!" he said firmly.

"I thought it was realism?"

"Yes realism, but it is symbolic realism!" he responded immediately, with the confidence of someone who has the right answer to this precise objection.

"What about socialist realism?"

"No, that does not work here! That kind works in socialist countries!" he answered promptly.

"What about psychological realism?"

"What?" he cried out, as if he were stung by a bee. "Do you mean that Freudian nonsense? Is that really what you think we need at this important era of our cause?"

"Magical realism?" I suggested in an imploring tone of voice, making my final bid for a different kind of realism. But no chance!

"That would weaken the political message of the play!"

He went on, and I nearly asked him which fucking political message he was on about. But I did not, fearing that he would certainly get upset and refuse to enquire after Salim.

And then I remembered Salim. I remembered his theory about the origin of magical realism. He came to see me one day. He had just finished reading *The Picture of Dorian Gray*, and loved it very much.

"Do you know who is the father of magical realism?" he asked me in an excited voice.

We were sitting in that café where the owner nearly had a heart attack every time he saw us coming into his shop.

"Márquez, Cortázar, Borges, Llosa ..." I went on naming every single Latin American writer that I had ever heard of.

"No, no! Oscar Wilde!" he interrupted me with a big foolish grin on his face.

"Oscar Wilde?"

"Yes. Oscar Wilde," he confirmed, getting closer to me as if he had intended to confide a deep secret. "On what do signs of decay and corruption appear in the course of the story?"

I did not understand. What did this have to do with magical realism? And he did not fail to notice how baffled I was.

"On the picture itself!" he rushed to say.

"I don't understand."

"Not on the guy himself," he went on explaining with an impatient voice, "I mean, not on the face of Dorian Gray, but on his picture. Imagine it, it is the image of the man, not the man himself that grows old and corrupt!"

"Ha, ha!" I hummed, not that I understood much, but I thought that that was getting interesting.

"Ha, ha! The story in general is a story of realist outlook, but this particular thing about the picture, makes the whole story a combination of the real and the fantastic, just as it is supposed to be in magical realism!"

Having explained his theory of the origin of magical realism to his own satisfaction, he sat back in his chair, as if to leave me a space to think and respond to him.

"So you think that magical realism is the combination of fantasy and reality?"

"Of course!"

"'Of course!'" I repeated, mockingly, and asked after a pause, "do you want my honest opinion?"

He nodded.

"Yes?" I asked, and couldn't help telling him what I thought exactly: "Shit on you, and on Oscar Wilde and magical realism and everyone who taught you to read the novel in this way!"

I remembered now the look of disappointment on his face. I felt guilty, and hated myself. Salim was good to me, yet with my usual arrogance I could not be sympathetic to him and show some appreciation of that funny theory of his.

I hated myself. And as if in repentance, I went on imploring Ahmad to do whatever he could so Salim would not be arrested. It was no longer my fear of losing the only source of cannabis and tablets that urged me to help him, but a deep sense of guilt for not having been friendly to him. I was overcome with emotion and at that very moment I determined to arrange a date with Dalal for him.

Salim loved Dalal, and wanted to sleep with her. And I was surprised and disappointed. He was a good looking man, but she looked like a monkey. What made it even worse was that she did not like him. She used to look down on him and make fun of the way he spoke. His unusual Iraqi accent made her laugh, and she often mocked him in his absence. I used to get angry. And the last time she mocked him in front of me I told her off. She cried and said that I did not understand. But I did. I understood only too well. She loved me, and hoped that one day we could get married. But every time she cried and said things like that, I thought to myself, that was exactly what I needed for my life to be a total disaster: to remain in Lebanon and get married to a monkey.

Sitting in the café, I remembered Dalal and shook my head in despair. But then I realised that if I really wanted to organise a date between Salim and her, I should first make it up with her. I could not persuade her that Salim was the man for her, I thought to myself, before I had apologised to her and told her how much I admired her. It was Salim who was madly in love with her, I would tell her, and it was he alone who would make her eternally happy. Yes! I thought of telling her all that, and perhaps quoting a few lines from the poems that Salim had written about her.

Sitting in that café, I remembered how Salim

read to me the poems he had written about Dalal. The man was a madman, I thought to myself, and decided to go and see her the next day. But I didn't. I neither went the next day nor the day after, nor the day after that. To be honest, I don't remember when I finally managed to go. I was getting ever more confused because of those damned tablets that I used to take.

VI

Eventually I went to the Camp and saw her.

I had to wait in front of the grocery shop opposite her home. The grocer kept eyeing me suspiciously, but I ignored him. I waited for a long time. And while waiting, a man whom I didn't remember I had ever seen before came to me and shook my hand. He told me that he had been looking for me all over the Camp and the city. He said he had finished the book that he had told me about, and that he was in urgent need of the opinion of an intellectual like me. He added, after a pause, that in the whole Camp one could never find a decent intellectual.

I was flattered.

And I loved to be flattered. But I did not remember his book, nor did I remember him. Noticing my confusion, he went on trying to remind me of the book.

"The book I told you about when we met at Abu Ramzi's?"

No, I did not remember. However, I remembered Abu Ramzi. I remembered that he was living alone after his wife had run away with a young man from the West Bank. I thought it would be perfect if I could meet Dalal at Abu Ramzi's house. It was there where we could have a chance to talk without fear of being seen by her family or her relatives or her neighbours.

Abu Ramzi was a good man. He understood the situation completely, as he assured me every time I had to stay at his place. Whenever I had a row with my family I went to him and he would say immediately: "I understand the situation, I understand!" and point to an empty room where I could spend the night peacefully.

"Don't you remember?" asked that person again. "Don't you remember my book? The one on the class structure of the Palestinian Revolution?"

"Aaah!" I exclaimed, pretending that I had remembered, and that everything had become crystal clear to me.

Encouraged by this "aaah", the fellow went on telling me more about his study, with a big smile on his face. But I didn't hear a single word of what he was saying. I was busy waiting for Dalal to appear. Luckily I did not wait for long, for soon she came out of her house and headed towards a nearby alley.

I said goodbye to that person whom I never managed to remember, telling him, by way of an apology for leaving so hastily, that I was ever so interested in his book and must read it. Striding away, I told him that I would be grateful if he could provide me with a copy of that important study of his.

"Yes, of course, but at what address?" he cried.

I hadn't really thought of that, and didn't know what to say. But all of a sudden I pointed to the grocery shop: "Here! Leave a copy for me with the grocer, he is my friend," I cried out while crossing the road, rushing towards the alley into which Dalal had just gone. Dalal had seen me, but did not stop. I followed her, leaving a few steps between us until I was certain that we had gone far enough from her home and that we could no longer been seen by either her family or neighbours. I told her that I must talk to her on an important matter, and hurried up, beckoning to her to follow me.

At first she ignored me and kept walking slowly as if to prove to me she was not really interested in what I was going to say, but as soon as she saw me striding away, not willing to stop and imploring her to come with me, she started to hurry up, trying to catch up with me.

In a few minutes I reached Abu Ramzi's house. I knocked at the door, and stood there, watching Dalal approaching with a tilted head.

"God, she really is an ugly bitch!" I said to myself.

Abu Ramzi came to the door and I tried to explain, but he interrupted me saying that he understood the situation perfectly well, and led us through, pointing to one of the empty rooms. He showed no curiosity in my companion, and I was relieved. Who on earth would want to look at Dalal's face? I thought to myself.

Abu Ramzi was living alone in this large house. People claimed that after his wife had run away he vowed not to leave the house again. But people used to say many things. Dalal said that she did not like it here. She said that if she were seen entering or leaving Abu Ramzi's house people would start gossiping about her all over the Camp. She looked shy at being alone with me, but I felt that she was only pretending. Dalal was not the sort of girl who would be shy at being alone with a man. Everybody knew that.

I got close to her, and pinched her. She laughed and pinched me. I slapped her bare arm, and she slapped mine. I bit her neck and she bit mine, and soon we were lying on the carpeted floor, her head on my shoulder. At that moment, I thought to myself, why on earth am I thinking of going to

Germany? Why don't I stay here, and marry this monkey? I could sleep with her every night, and in no time we could have ten children. We could row every day until Israel comes back again and destroys this fucking Camp all over our heads so we die and that would be that.

I had forgotten the purpose of bringing Dalal here.

I had forgotten Salim, and my attempt to sort things out between him and Dalal.

I had forgotten how worried I was about him and how guilty I felt.

VII

I forgot Salim until I saw Ahmad, days, or perhaps, weeks later.

He rushed into the café, brushing drops of rain off his large coat and smoothing his soaked hair.

It was raining heavily outside. And I thought that Ahmad was rushing trying to seek shelter from the rain, but he did not stay for long. He stood by the table, breathing heavily, and told me the news.

"They have arrested Salim!" he said and went on looking left and right.

"Who? When?"

"Who do you think?" he exclaimed impatiently and turned back, looking towards the door of the café. He obviously was in hurry, and before I managed to ask him to sit down, he said that he had come only to tell me of Salim's arrest. I tried to find out more, but he said that he could not stay, and that he would come the day after. Waving, he turned and strode towards the entrance.

"What about the play?" I shouted.

"Not now, not now!" he cried, striding out at the same speed he had come in.

I looked around, and saw the owner of the café, watching us and shaking his head in despair.

Ahmad's behaviour baffled me. It was not like him to waste an opportunity to talk about a matter of great concern, especially his play. But my confusion did not last long. Soon Abu Shivan appeared at the door. Looking left and right, staring at the faces of the customers, he walked in. I realised he was looking for Ahmad. And I nearly burst out laughing, but I was worried that the owner of the café would have a heart attack.

As soon as Abu Shivan caught sight of me, he rushed towards me with a speed that did not fit his huge body. He looked funny, and I thought that his bulk must be a surplus of food supply that he stole. For some reason I wished that one day he would choke to death on the food that he had been stealing.

"Have you seen Ahmad?" he asked breathlessly, and before saying hello.

"No!" I replied curtly, turning my face aside. I was worried that he might catch me staring at his big belly.

"No! Are you sure?"

"Absolutely sure, I have not seen him for two weeks."

He was astonished, and went on looking around. Letting out a big sigh, he pulled up the chair opposite me and rested himself down.

"Do you know what your friend Ahmad has done?" asked Abu Shivan in a voice of someone who had suffered great disappointment.

I stared at him with disgust, but said nothing.

"He cheated me out of fifty thousand liras!"

"Forty thousand," I corrected him calmly, and thought at that very moment that I should go to see the travel agent.

"Yes, yes, forty thousand!" he rushed to correct himself in an apologetic voice. "But how did you know? Did he tell you?"

I did not reply.

I was worried, thinking about that crook of a travel agent who promised to get me a visa to Germany. I was also worried about Salim. I thought that he might get killed and decided to find a way of saving him from Abu Omar and his men.

"For two months now he's been promising me to print a newspaper for the party," Abu Shivan went on, "but until now he has not produced a single scrap of printed paper. He took the money and came back with no result whatsoever."

Of course, Abu Shivan was expecting me to condemn what Ahmad had done, but I kept silent. I was more concerned with finding a way of rescuing Salim.

"Comrade Bassem!" Abu Shivan addressed me by my first name. He must have noticed that I was thinking of something else, and tried to engage my attention again.

"Comrade Bassem! You are an educated man and you must know how important it is for our party to have a newspaper of its own. In fact it is very important not for our party only, but for the Kurdish cause as a whole."

"Yes, yes!" I agreed, but only to prove to him that I was still listening to every word he had to say.

"Comrade Bassem, the Kurdish cause is the twin sister of the Palestinian cause, and what Ahmad has done is a stab in the back of the two causes together!"

No, it is a stab to your pocket, you frozen-chicken thief! I thought to myself. And then I thought about the travel agent who took fifty thousand from me for the mere promise of getting me a visa to Germany. And I said to myself that I should stop being lazy and go to see him. If he hadn't got me the visa, I would simply ask him to pay back my money. But then I thought that first I must try to save Salim.

"Try to convince him to do that paper for us," Abu Shivan was begging me now, "or at least to give me my money back. I have cut it out of my children's food!"

No you haven't, I thought to myself, you have cut it out of the salaries of your men, you little thief!

He must have realised that I was not so keen to listen to any more of his complaints. He remained silent for a while, and rose slowly, claiming that he had urgent political tasks to attend to.

"Are you going to the Camp?" I asked with an unexpectedly friendly voice.

He nodded.

"Can you give me a lift?" I asked, and added right away, "I'll try to find Ahmad and talk to him."

I had no intention of talking to Ahmad, least of all about Abu Shivan's little worry. All I wanted was to get a lift to the Camp. And I thought if I did not claim that I was going to talk to Ahmad, Abu Shivan would have never agreed to take me there. Or he might agree but on the condition of paying a fare. I had heard what a cheap bastard he was, and feared that once we arrived at the Camp, Abu Shivan would exclaim in a cab driver's voice, "That will be fifty liras, please!"

Abu Shivan was a greedy bastard, but once he believed that I was going to the Camp for his sake alone he was happy to offer me a lift.

VIII

It was still raining. Pools of water stretched across the roads all the way to the Camp. I kept thanking Providence for giving the Palestinian cause a twin sister like the Kurdish cause and for giving the Kurdish cause a political party like the KLP, and giving the KLP a leader like Abu Shivan who had a car and was giving me a lift and saving me from being soaked with rain. I thought that if Ahmad had heard me saying things like that, he would've gone berserk.

"It's martyrs' blood, the money which is being wasted on parasites like Abu Shivan!" Ahmad often said when ever he heard that some new leader of a newly founded party had obtained a budget from Fatah. "Martyrs' blood is being turned into wasted money on mercenaries," Ahmad used to say.

I thought that Ahmad obviously did not believe

that supporting the KLP was necessarily support for the Kurdish cause, the twin sister of our own. I even thought that by swindling Abu Shivan, Ahmad must have been trying, in some way, to retrieve the blood of the martyrs which had been wasted. However, Ahmad was retrieving it, and tucking it into his own pocket. What a little devil you are, my dear Ahmad, I thought to myself.

And at once, I thought I must go and see the travel agent who had promised me, in a highly confident manner, to secure my route to Germany. Then I thought I must first try to save Salim.

But all of a sudden I noticed that I kept saying that I must save Salim. Who the hell was I? I asked myself, the Scarlet Pimpernel? The brave knight who saved members of the French nobility from the guillotine of the French Revolution? But then I started wondering whether we could consider the French Revolution the eldest sister of our own Revolution. And I went on thinking of who might be, in this case, the youngest sister. The Iranian Revolution, perhaps? Then I thought that our Revolution had too many siblings. What madness, I thought, and shook my head as if to brush away the idiotic thoughts that I had.

It was still raining, and I strode away.

I had decided to go to see Abu Al-Ezz, and seek his help to release Salim. Abu Al-Ezz was a well-known military leader and no political or military head in the area would dare to refuse him a request.

I remembered once when PSF, the Popular Struggle Front, kidnapped a young Christian man from Magdosha. The parents of the guy came to Abu Al-Ezz and begged him to try to release their son. Abu Al-Ezz did not fail them in spite of the great cost that had to be paid.

He immediately phoned up Abu Al-Hawel, the leader of PSF, and told him to let the young man go without any delay. But Abu Al-Hawel refused, claiming that the kidnapped man was a Mossad agent. Abu Al-Ezz assured him that the guy was not a Mossad agent, and that everybody in Magdosha knew that he and his family were the best people in the village. But Abu Al-Hawel would not budge. What's worse, he told Abu Al-Ezz that he was not willing to free an Israeli spy, so he, Abu Al-Ezz, could show off in front of his friends in Magdosha and be invited to their homes where he could have a drink while staring at their women.

Abu Al-Ezz went berserk. And he swore in front of everybody that he was not only going to free the prisoner, but also teach Abu Al-Hawel a lesson which he could never forget.

It wasn't the first time that a leader of one faction had sworn to teach another a lesson. Leaders of factions and parties in the Camp often taught each other unforgettable lessons. And Abu Al-Ezz nearly succeeded in doing just that in the same day, but at the last moment things took a different turn. And just when Abu Al-Ezz was about to take over the HQ of the PSF, release the kidnapped man and finish Abu Al-Hawel off, other factions and parties intervened, demanding the immediate withdrawal of Abu Al-Ezz's forces. Of course Abu Al-Ezz realised that he had no chance against so many united factions, and considered withdrawing. Fortunately other factions came on to his help. Soon the battle was no longer between Abu Al-Ezz and Abu Al-Hawel, but between all factions.

A battle erupted on every conceivable front in the Camp. At first, machine-guns were used, but soon fighters resorted to heavier sorts of armour. Fighting went on for three days non-stop. Five people were killed, and twenty-four were wounded. And as usual, those who were killed, had their photos in huge posters attached to the walls of the Camp, and under each photo was written, the familiar brief obituary: The hero martyr so and so, was born in such and such a place. And he was martyred in a heroic confrontation with the Zionist enemy.

If it hadn't been for orders coming from HQ in Tunisia, the war would have gone on and on. More people would have been killed and wounded and more posters would've been glued to the walls of the Camp.

Abu Al-Ezz, however, was very pleased with the outcome of the battle. He had succeeded in raiding the offices of PSF and freeing the kidnapped man. He had also managed to arrest all the members of that organisation, including Abu Al-Hawel. And he went on boasting, in front of the people of Magdosha, that Abu Al-Hawel had sought his forgiveness, kissing his hand and imploring him to spare him his life.

Abu Al-Ezz had gone by himself to Magdosha, to return the newly freed man safely. The parents of the freed man, and also people of the village, thanked him warmly but expressed their dismay and sorrow that a battle was fought, and innocent civilians were killed and injured. But Abu Al-Ezz assured them that there was nothing for them to feel guilty about. What had happened, he added in a sombre voice, had to happen. For a long time, he said, he had been waiting for the right opportunity to teach Abu Al-Hawel a lesson that he could not forget and now he'd had his opportunity.

He was thanked once and twice and thrice. The mother of the freed man kissed him on the cheek, and he blushed. And people invited him for a drink, which he accepted gratefully.

He sat among them, sipping his arak, and staring at the women.

Remembering what happened then, I grew hopeful. If Abu Al-Ezz, I said to myself, had fought a hard battle for the sake of friends in Magdosha, then he would certainly fight a harder battle for the sake of my family, and to honour his friendship with my uncle.

Abu Al-Ezz was a good friend of my family, but particularly my uncle. He often visited us when were still living in the Camp. I was only seven then. He and my uncle were in the same political party, were also friends, and remained so even after my uncle had left the party and went to America to continue his studies. Abu Al-Ezz was disappointed that my uncle had decided to abandon the route of political struggle and attend to his personal ambition. But as time went by, Abu Al-Ezz became more envious than disappointed, especially when he gradually heard that my uncle had managed to get a degree, get a job, get married to an American woman and acquire American citizenship.

I was certain that Abu Al-Ezz would do his best to release Salim. I thought it would be enough for me to tell him that Salim was one of those warriors who had been with the Revolution from the beginning, and that he had fought in the "War of the Mountain", and was seriously injured. I thought that once I said this to Abu Al-Ezz he would rush to contact Abu Omar and demand the release of Salim immediately.

Abu Al-Ezz himself had fought in the War of

the Mountain. He often boasted about that, and regretted the passing of those days when fighting had a meaning.

I was sure that Abu Al-Ezz was the man to set Salim free. And I was glad that I had decided to go and see him.

But, strangely enough, I did not go after all.

Suddenly while walking in the rain, I changed my mind and went to see Dalal again instead.

I stood in front the grocery shop opposite her home, and waited until she emerged and saw me. At the beginning the bitch ignored me, but I called her, and we went together to Abu Ramzi's house. I knew that Abu Ramzi would not mind. He would understand the situation, as he often did, and let us into one of the empty rooms.

We went to Abu Ramzi, and there I pinched Dalal and she pinched me, I slapped her bare arm and she slapped mine. I bit her and she bit me, and then we lay down on the faded carpeted floor.

IX

I forgot all about Salim.

I don't know how I was able to forget him. Suddenly Salim became a mere name of someone that I could scarcely remember. Even when

Ahmad told me the terrible news, I didn't feel greater sadness or anger than I would have felt had Salim been a perfect stranger.

Ahmad told me that Salim had been murdered and I was not shocked. I didn't feel angry or sad. I just nodded as if Ahmad was merely telling me something trivial, in which I had no great interest. Ahmad looked baffled. Apparently he had thought deep and long before he brought himself to tell me the bad news. He obviously did not want to shock me, so he tried his best to break the news as gently as he could. But now it was he who was shocked and confused.

I had begged him to enquire after Salim and then I behaved as if the matter was of very little interest to me. At first Ahmad assumed that the shock was so great for me that I was unable to express how I felt. But I was not shocked, and I made sure that Ahmad knew that I was not.

I simply no longer cared about what had happened to Salim.

We were sitting in the café. The owner of the café, however, was not there. The waiter told us that he was in hospital. And I thought that must have happened because of us. The man could no longer stand our presence and had fallen ill.

Ahmad resumed talking about Salim. He was not convinced that I did not care, and he wanted to bring out my feelings. He himself could not stand the likes of Salim, but he must have thought one should show some sympathy when death is involved. He told me that Salim had been tortured. He also told me that Salim had confessed that he had broken into houses of leaders of parties and factions in the Camp and some times into military bases and ammunition stores. Salim had confessed that he once sneaked into a military base while everybody was asleep, including the sentry. He had collected every single weapon he could lay hands on and sold them. Ahmad went on, in a rather sarcastic tone of voice, telling me how Salim used to sell stolen weapons to whoever wished to buy, for whatever money he was offered. Once Ahmad said that, he seemed to have lost his feigned sense of regret over Salim's death. He actually started lamenting the fact that the Revolution had become a home for the likes of Salim. I felt that he was about to start swearing at the cause of it all, the Walking Disaster, Arafat, but all of a sudden, he drew back. He must have realised that was not the time for him to talk as he usually did. At that moment I wished he would have stopped. But no, he resumed expressing his sorrow for the death of Salim, "that young man", as he put it, who was doomed to die far away from his family and country.

Luckily, he fell silent. He stared at me to see what effect his words had had on me, but was no less confused. What he had said had no effect on me. In fact I was getting bored, and wanted to change the subject as soon as possible.

"How is the play going?"

"What?" he asked in astonishment, as if to tell me that this was not the time to talk about the play.

But he soon relaxed. And I knew that even if the dead man were a close relation of his, he wouldn't have wasted an opportunity to talk about the play, or anything of the slightest relevance to our fucking cause.

With a look of excitement on his face, he told me that the date had been set for the opening night. He went on, in some detail, telling me of the final rehearsals and how everything looked, just as he had imagined it and planned it. Encouraged, probably, by the fact that that was the first time I had shown serious interest in his play, Ahmad declared that he had never been, in his entire life, as right about something as in choosing Al-nidal Artistic Company to perform the play. I nearly told him that Al-nidal Artistic Company was as talented as a herd of cows in a desert, but I was worried that he might stop talking about the play and go back to talking about Salim.

He claimed that the director had shown such an impressive sensitivity to the hidden political and artistic messages of the play, and boasted that it was so and so, an actress, who was going to play the role of Om Saad. She had appeared in many television dramas, he said, and was perfect for the role. As for the role of Saad, he declared, with total satisfaction, that it could have never been played the way it was going to be played by the young actor so and so who was deemed to have a bright future in the artistic world. And it was such and such a person who was going to play the role of the Mokhtar. I had never heard of the actors mentioned, but Ahmad was talking about them as if they were popular icons.

"Art! Art! That is what is going to save us from the degenerate state we are living in!" he declared, choking in his overjoyed tone of voice.

"What about the *intifada*?" I asked, trying to point out to him that in his state of total happiness over the play he was producing, he had forgotten all about the *intifada*. He used to consider the *intifada* as the only hopeful response to the state of corruption that we were suffering.

"Of course, the *intifada*, as well," he replied cheerfully, as if a fortune had just fallen into his lap. "But you must know, the *intifada* is in itself a work of art," he added, after a pause, with a great look of satisfaction lightening up his face.

I felt that this look was not the result of being able to answer a tricky question, but rather of being so eloquent in his response. But his happiness did not last long. He stared at me, hoping that I would be impressed. But I was not. I actually looked at him in disgust as if he had just farted from his mouth.

Ahmad was disappointed and embarrassed. He started fumbling in the pockets of his large coat, and took out a thick envelope. He opened it and pulled out two white tickets, and handed them to me.

"One for you, and one for a friend, if you wish to bring a friend along!" he said, still sulking.

They were tickets for the play, and I started reading what was written on them, but before I had finished he hastened to say that the opening night was on the following Thursday.

"Seven o'clock, don't forget!" he said in a tone of voice which implied that he expected me to forget or to find an excuse for not attending.

I thought that he was trying to get his own back for my disappointing him earlier, but I promised him that I would attend. I told him that on that particular day I was going to see the travel agent first, and would join him later at the theatre door.

"Are you still determined to leave?" Ahmad asked in a sad tone of voice.

I liked that. I liked the way he sounded. I had never thought that anybody would be sad to see me leave the country. Not even my own family. On the contrary, I thought that my family would feel relieved to see the back of me. As for the leader of my party, he could not be happier than to get rid of me, and save the salary he paid me from his budget. Of course he would try to conceal his delight, not by pretending to be sorry, but by claiming that he was sure that by going to Germany I was not aiming to give up political activity altogether. For reasons known only to himself, he would be absolutely certain that once I had settled in Germany I would try to found a branch of the party over there. I wouldn't have been surprised if he actually expected me to do so. For the leader of our party had often boasted about "our comrades" who had gone to this or that country and established new branches, which gradually became some of the biggest ones of the party as a whole. Though everybody knew for certain that our party was no bigger that Abu Shivan's, the leader did not have a shred of doubt that the party had friends and allies all over the world.

I had often heard him claiming that "our comrades" were playing a major role in the *intifada*, and that "our comrades" in Moscow were performing such an extraordinary task among Palestinian students that they had even impressed our Soviet comrades. Whenever I heard him saying that, I thought that he must have been hoping to meet Gorbachev himself.

"What a loss! What a loss!" Ahmad went on, shaking his head. "One day after another we lose a revolutionary asset."

I was stunned by this statement, and looked at him to see whether he was being serious or just making fun of my leaving the country. I had never believed, not for one second, that I was an asset of any sort, let alone a revolutionary asset. The tablets that I had been taking had made me so weak and forgetful that sometimes I did not know where I was going to, nor coming from, nor whether, in the first place, I was going or coming.

I wished that Ahmad would stop lamenting my going away. Luckily I remembered Abu Shivan. I remembered that Abu Shivan was looking for him. I knew that that would make him forget all about me and my intention to go away. I asked him if he had seen Abu Shivan. But he pretended not to understand. I told him that Abu Shivan was looking for him in order to retrieve the fifty thousand liras that he had taken from him. I deliberately said fifty thousand in order to have his full reaction. And just as I had expected, he went mad. He started swearing at Abu Shivan and his shitty party, the Revolution which had become a nest of scum, and of course Arafat, who had taken in every crook that had been creeping on the face of the earth. He shook his head, and went on lamenting martyrs' spirits whose blood had been wasted on parasites and vagabonds from all over the world. He insisted on telling me the whole story.

He said that Abu Shivan did not give him more than forty thousand liras. And that he had to buy so many materials in order to produce that fucking newsletter. Getting all worked up again, he swore that the amount of money he had received was not even enough to buy the required materials, and that he had to pay for the rest out of his own pocket. And he carried on swearing about Abu Shivan, and explained that the only reason he couldn't produce the newsletter was because he could not find one single Kurd who could write. Abu Shivan himself, he claimed, was an illiterate.

"What did he expect from me?" asked Ahmad, "to write in Kurdish?" And again, he started swearing about Abu Shivan, the Kurds, the Palestinians and the fucker Arafat. He vowed that he could never rest until he got the bastard Abu Shivan out of the Camp.

"From now on, I shall devote myself to achieving nothing but this goal!" Ahmad said. "The bastard has been going from one place to another smearing my reputation."

I was overjoyed, and tried my best not to burst out laughing. Here Ahmad was at his best, I said to myself. I really liked listening to Ahmad. And at that moment, I thought, if I ever managed to leave the country, the only person that I was going to miss was Ahmad. Where on earth would I find another Ahmad? I grew sad. But deep down I

knew that the moment I would leave this country
I would forget everybody and everything. I should
forget Ahmad before forgetting anyone else. And if
I should remember him at all, I would remember
him just as a sort of joke. I had already forgotten
Salim while I was still there, so why shouldn't I
forget Ahmad the moment I left? Yes, I thought to
myself, I shall go to Germany and work as a pimp in
a brothel and forget Ahmad and all the people I knew.

I said to myself that one should forget. Luckily I
had been taking enough tablets to make me forget
without even trying. But then I was thinking of all
the people that I knew, people I loved and people I
hated. And oh my God how many people I hated
and wished that they would vanish off the face of
the earth, so I did not have to see them again.

X

I went out, leaving Ahmad, sitting alone in the
café.

I went walking aimlessly; a nauseous feeling had
taken over me and a sound of banging went on in my
head. It was banging and banging, and it was so
noisy that it distracted me from everything else.

I thought first that I should go home, and try
to sleep it off, but the thought itself made it worse.

I thought if I went home, while I was in that state, I would've killed the lot of them without any sense of shame or guilt. I imagined myself entering the house and finding them fighting again, and without saying a word I would go to the bedroom, bring out the Kalashinkov and shoot them all at once.

I would shoot them, and go to the kitchen to make myself a cup of coffee. Perhaps I should shoot myself as well, and better still, go to the next-door neighours and shoot them, and then shoot myself. They also were sons of bitches who deserved to die.

At that moment I wanted to open fire at some-one, and I remembered the travel agent. I thought that I should go to see him and ask him whether he had got me the visa. If he hadn't, I would shoot him on the spot. It sounded so appropriate that I immediately strode in the direction of his office. But then I realised that I did not have a gun. I decided to go home first, get the gun and then go to see that crook. I turned and started walking towards home. But I didn't walk on for long. I was seriously worried that if I entered the house in that state of mind, I wouldn't leave before I had killed everybody in it.

I stopped in the middle of the road, not knowing where to go or what to do. I said to myself that I must have gone mad. I liked the idea that I had gone mad, and thought that I was in a similar situation to that of Hamlet's: to walk or not to walk, that was the fucking question. I decided to write a poem:

Hamlet, you noble soul
Glory to your name
But, if you had been living in this country
You would have become a bastard,
A revolutionary pimp,
Or a fucker of a freedom fighter!

But then I had an erection, and I thought that was a good sign, and that from then on everything would be just right.

I decided to go and see Dalal.

And I went to Dalal, and then we went together to Abu Ramzi's house. Abu Ramzi told us: "I understand the situation, I understand!" and led us to one of the empty rooms.

And we slept.

I slept.

In fact I fell into a deep sleep and dreamt that I was in hell and had just met the devil. I kissed his feet, and his feet had a similar smell to Dalal's body. I sought his forgiveness, but he said that he would only forgive me if I continued that poem.

I begged him and told him that I didn't like poetry. I did not like poets and thought that they were all a bunch of parasites, and if it were up to me I would've detained them in a labour camp and made them work for their living. The devil agreed with me, and promised to look into the matter, but he insisted that I should finish the poem first. He gave me some paper and I withdrew into a corner, and started racking my brain trying to complete the poem.

Oh, noble, Hamlet,
Glory to your name,
But if you had been in this country ...

But I fell asleep. I slept deeply and dreamt that I was sitting with Ahmad in the café. I dreamt that the owner of the café was shouting at us: "Get off my back, you sons of a bitches!"

We didn't hear him. I was listening to Ahmad. He was busy explaining to me the importance of realism in this particular era of the history of our just cause. I tried to convince him that realism was the art of failures, but he insisted that it was the proper style to represent our just cause. I got all fed up and told him to shove our just cause up his arse.

I thought I could write another poem, called "A just cause up my friend Ahmad's bottom".

But I slept deeply. I was actually descending from one layer of sleep to a lower layer. I thought I was on my way to death. But then I realised that I was already dead. And I asked myself, do the dead die?

I thought that such a question could be a good topic of discussion among Arab intellectuals. A journalist from a stupid newspaper could take up the issue: do the dead die?

Intellectual number one: What is this non-sense? There is an *intifada* going on, there are children confronting the Zionist enemy with their bare chests, and you are asking such an absurd question.

Intellectual number two: In my opinion there is death in life and life in death. In fact death is an aspect of life, and life is an aspect of death ...

Intellectual number three: I think we should first deconstruct the question, "do the dead die?"

Intellectual number four: Allah, the Almighty, says in the Koran ...

"Thank you very much," the journalist interrupts him, and walks away.

XI

But I did not die.

I woke up in the morning with a terrible hangover. I left the room and went to Abu Ramzi's. His face appeared from the half-opened door, peaceful and friendly, and I felt safe. I asked him what day it was.

"Friday," he said, without any trace of surprise or astonishment.

I realised that I had slept for three days on end, and felt so ashamed. I wanted to apologise to Abu Ramzi, but he rushed to say that he completely understood the situation. And I was encouraged by his understanding and asked if I could have a bath. He nodded. I went to the bathroom, and thought, while washing, that Abu Ramzi was really a good man, and that he really meant what he said whenever he said that he understood the situation.

Yes, I thought to myself, he understood the situation perfectly well. But this was an unbearable situation, which should not go on for long. I decided to go and see the travel agent right away. I must know for sure whether he had managed to obtain for me a visa to Germany or not. I must, I said to myself while still bathing, be frank with him and tell him that I was not expecting miracles. If he had not succeeded in getting me a visa to Germany, I was willing to accept any visa to any other country. I should be honest with him, and tell him that I was willing to take any route that leads out of this country. For a moment I grew calm. But my calmness did not last for long. Soon doubts crept into my mind. What if, I wondered, no country in the world gave me a visa? What if the embassies of the whole world closed their doors in my face?

"We cannot accept a person like you!" staff of embassies would tell me one after another.

"You must stay here!" one member of staff would say.

"You must die here!" another member of staff would say.

I quickly put on my clothes, and set out to see the travel agent without any further delay. I desperately needed some assurance that at least one country in the world was willing to accept me. I wanted to hear the travel agent telling me that there were many embassies that would grant me a visa. I wanted to hear it, even if it was a mere lie. What the hell? I thought. And I was calm and joyful and felt like whistling - but I did not know how to whistle.

"But could my joy last for long? Could I be happy for more than a few minutes? No, certainly not!" I said to myself the moment I reached the travel agency and discovered that it had been closed down.

"I have been doomed since the day I was born," I said to myself. I enjoyed telling myself things like this whenever I faced a predicament. And what worse a predicament could there be than the one I was facing then. The door of the travel agency was blocked with timber, and on one side there was a typed piece of paper which informed those who were concerned - people like me of course - that the office was closed down by the police and that those who had any query should go to the police station at such and such a street. I didn't need the brain of a genius to figure out what had happened. The travel agent, just as I had thought from the beginning, was a crook. He had collected from the likes of me as much money as he could and run away. It was an ordinary tale that did not deserve to be mentioned even in the local press.

I was angry and sad. And I cried. I cried until tears ran down my cheeks. People in the street looked at me and thought that I had just come out of the cinema, and I had seen an Indian film the tragic story of which had torn my heart apart. How could anybody cry in that way if he hadn't seen an Indian film?

I was so sad, and cried. But then I was glad, and laughed too. I was glad because I realised that from the beginning I was right about the travel agent. I had not been right about anything for the last few years, but now at last, I had managed to get something right. I had known that the travel agent was a crook, and he turned out to be just the way I had thought he was.

I was happy and thought of going home to share my happiness with my family. I could tell them how right I was, and they would be so happy and proud of a son like me. Yes, I was glad and laughed. I let out a great hysterical laugh and people looked at me and thought that I had gone mad. I walked down towards the café while I was still laughing. I had decided to tell Ahmad what had happened, and we could both laugh together. Ahmad, I thought to myself, did not lack a sense of humour. Though he kept talking nonsense about our shitty cause, he appreciated a good joke when he heard one.

I kept laughing, but when I reached the café, I stopped. It seemed that something had happened. I saw a crowd of people, and a military vehicle parked in front of the café. As I got closer, I noticed that the glass window was shattered. Tables and chairs were turned upside-down. I looked around, trying to find someone of the regular customers that I knew. I saw Ahmad among the onlookers, and made my way towards him. He rushed to tell me that the owner of the café had gone mad. He had thrown the customers out and started wrecking the place. But a man who was standing nearby interrupted, and told us that the owner had discovered that he had been robbed. He had gone to the toilet for a few minutes, and when he came back he found the till empty. He could not take it and went berserk. Another person told us that the story of the robbery was not true. The fact, he said, was that the man was ill. He had been in hospital for several weeks, and since he came out he had been accusing everyone of robbing him. A third person said that the man had got fed up with the café, and that was what had caused his illness in the first place.

There were other people saying other things. But I said to myself that it was our frequenting the café that made him fed up with the café and life itself.

XII

"Let's go!" Ahmad said, shaking his head in sorrow.

We strolled away, and he said after a pause that he knew another café, where we could go presently, and where we could possibly go regularly in the future. And I wished to ask him what future he was talking about, but I kept silent.

We walked on silently, but suddenly Ahmad stopped and looked at me as if he had just noticed my presence.

"And what happened to you?" he asked.

I thought of telling him that I had slept for three days, but I knew he would not believe me. He probably would have thought that I was making fun of him. I told him about the travel agent, how he had made the swindle and disappeared. And by way of explaining my absence for the last three days, I said that I had been busy with this problem. And that was why, I added, I could not attend the opening night of the play. I was worried that he might question me further and discover that I was not telling the truth, so I rushed to ask him how the play went.

"Fine, fine!" he said curtly.

I suspected that things did not go as well as Ahmad had wished. And I was getting all excited and curious, and waited for him to tell me more. I knew that Ahmad would eventually tell me. For a moment I forgot my curiosity and felt sorry for him. He had put so much into it and had high hopes.

"You cannot imagine the poor taste of some people," he said all of a sudden, sighing heavily.

"Oh, yes I know," I said, trying to encourage him to go on talking.

"You see the play went on very successfully, and everybody liked it," he said, "but there was a handful of hooligans who tried to spoil everything."

"Why? What happened?"

He told me that a small group of the audience kept jeering and making sarcastic remarks all through the play. Every time the fedayeen appeared on the stage, they jeered, "Here come the heroes, here come the heroes!" and when, at the end of the play, Om Saad asked her son, "If you and your friends do not fight to liberate Palestine, who would?" one replied, "We can always import Kurds!"

"Can you imagine the level of cynicism that some of us have reached?" Ahmad asked in a regretful tone of voice.

I was not trying to imagine anything at that moment. I was only trying to keep a straight face and I couldn't. I started chuckling, and raised my hand to my mouth to stop myself laughing.

Ahmad knew that I did not share his sense of disappointment. He went on shaking his head.

"We can import Kurds to liberate Palestine; that is a good one," I said. I was no longer able to control myself, and roared with laughter. Ahmad gave me a reproachful look, and I tried to cheer him up.

"Didn't I tell you that our cause has grown out of the phase of realism and has become surrealist?"

"Damn you!"

"Why?"

"Because you are as cynical as them," he said, and smiled.

And I was encouraged.

"Come on, you must appreciate the joke!" I said, and burst out laughing again.

"Yes, and what about you and that travel agent

who conned you?" he said sarcastically. "That was a good surrealist performance wasn't it?"

"Yes, everything has become surrealist now!" I said.

"You are such a fool," he said, "putting your trust in a swindler to get you to Germany!"

We both laughed. And I thought that since we were in such a joking mood I could tell Ahmad what had exactly happened to me in the last three days. I thought we could laugh more.

At the beginning Ahmad seemed amused, but as soon as I told him that I had dreamt that I was writing a poem titled "A Just Cause up the Bottom of my Friend Ahmad", he ceased laughing, and gave me a look of someone who was deeply offended.

"You are mad!" he shouted.

"And you are as a crooked as the travel agent and Abu Shivan as well!"

"Crooked? Like Abu Shivan? Me?" he said, and obviously was more surprised than offended.

"Yes, you are!" I said in a determined voice.

"Me?" he shouted again, and could no longer control himself. He punched me on the chin. It was so heavy a punch that I fell down.

"Damn you! You crook!" I shouted with pain and picked up a stone, and with all my strength I threw it at him. But I missed him. I tried to pick up another stone, but by then he had run away. I cursed him again, and then shouted at the top of my voice, "We can always import Kurds!"

I laughed. I laughed a great hysterical laugh.

Dusting down my clothes, I got up. I thought of going home to change, but instead, I decided to go and see Dalal, and a sense of sadness overcame me. And how was I not to be sad, if going to see Dalal was the only thing I could think of? I even thought of proposing marriage to her, and that was what made me even sadder.

Yes, I thought to myself, we must get married, Dalal and I. We will get married and have ten children, but then they will die, and have their photos as huge posters glued to the walls of the Camp, declaring them as heroic martyrs who have died while fighting the Zionist enemy. And Dalal and I would be the proud parents of ten martyrs. After that Israel could invade Lebanon again, destroy the Camp and fuck us all up, so we die and get the hell out of this fucking life.

XIII

It was getting dark when I reached the Camp. I heard cries coming from inside the elementary school.

"Beasts! Beasts!" came the cries of the little students in unison.

I climbed the wall of the school and looked into the playground. There were two rows of Cubs parading in a military fashion, while the trainer was walking up and down, and asking them in a strident voice, "Are you hungry?"

"Beasts!" the Cubs responded in voices no less loud and strident.

"Are you thirsty?" the trainer asked again.

"Beasts!" the Cubs shouted back in one voice.

I remembered that I was about to become a Cub once. I used to sneak out of the house, and go to the Cubs' training camp, where boys of my age used to gather and train to become Cubs. My father had forbidden me from going there. He did not like the fedayeen, and thought that they were a lazy lot. Once he caught me in the training camp. He was standing by the fence looking at me. I had no way to hide or run away. Anticipating the punishment that was awaiting me, I left the camp in silence and walked towards him with a bowed head. I thought that once I had reached him he would hold me by the lobe of my ear and haul me home where he would start thumping me with his huge and coarse hands and warning me that if I ever went there again he would put an end to my life.

But he did not.

As I got close to him he turned and walked in

front of me. I followed him, still frightened, and wondering what sort of punishment I was going to receive. But as we passed by an ice-cream vendor, he stopped and bought two big portions. He handed me one, and pointed to me to stand in the shade of a nearby house.

It was the largest portion of ice-cream that I had ever had.

I did not believe what was happening, and went on licking my ice-cream while eyeing him stealthily. He was standing there, in the middle of the road, eating his ice-cream and looking at something invisible at the end of the road.

When we finished, he came to me and asked in an unusually cordial voice, "do you want to go back to your friends?"

I nearly cried. I wanted to start running to the camp full of joy.

"No!" I said, "I want to go home with you." I wanted to please him.

"Let's go then!" he said, and looked at me, smiling.

"Beasts! Beasts!" I heard the Cubs crying out loud, and I was still looking over the wall of the school.

I felt thirsty. I felt thirsty and hungry. I nearly cried out, "I wish I were a Cub!"

But instead, I cried, "I wish I could leave this country!"

ACKNOWLEDGEMENTS

Etgar Keret's stories were translated from Hebrew by Miriam Shlesinger, except for "Shoes", by M. Weinberger-Rotman and "Missing Kissinger", by Dalya Bilu.

The English translations except "Cramps", "For Only 9.99" and "Gaza Blues" © the Institute for the Translation of Hebrew Lterature.

"For Only 9.99", "Shoshi", "Shoshi 2", "Shoshi 3" and "Vacuum Seal" were first published in Hebrew in *Pipelines*, Am Oved 1992. "Missing Kissinger" and "My Brother's Depressed" were first published in Hebrew in *Missing Kissinger*, Zmora Bitan, 1994. "Shooting Clint" and "Surprise Egg" were first published in Hebrew in *Anihu*, Zmora Bitan, 2002.

"Shoes", "Missing Kissinger", "Pipes" and "The Son of the Head of The Mossad" were first published in English in *The Bus Driver Who Wanted to be God*, St Martin's Press, New York, 2001.

"For Only 9.99", "Gaza Blues", "Crazy Glue", "Shoes", "Missing Kissinger", "The Son of the Head of the Mossad", "Pipes", "Cramps", "Shoshi", "Shoshi 2", "Shoshi 3", "Vacuum Seal", "My Brother's Depressed" © Etgar Keret.